THE HUNDRED WATERS

Also by Lauren Acampora

The Wonder Garden

The Paper Wasp

THE HUNDRED WATERS

A NOVEL

LAUREN ACAMPORA

Grove Press
New York

FIRST EDITION

Published simultaneously in Canada
Printed in Canada

First Grove Atlantic hardcover edition: August 2022

This book was set in 13.5-point Centaur MT by Alpha Design & Composition of Pittsfield, NH.

Library of Congress Cataloging-in-Publication data is available for this title.

ISBN 978-0-8021-5974-8
eISBN 978-0-8021-5975-5

Grove Press
an imprint of Grove Atlantic
154 West 14th Street
New York, NY 10011

Distributed by Publishers Group West

groveatlantic.com

22 23 24 25 26   10 9 8 7 6 5 4 3 2 1

*For my mother
and my daughter*

THE HUNDRED WATERS

I.

JUNE IN NEARWATER, Connecticut. Trees in bright leaf, juvenile green. From above, a pageant of growth. Only from the air can the true span of the estates be appreciated—the tennis courts, swimming pools, guesthouses—and the acres of wilderness between. At the far edge of town laps the Long Island Sound, past that, the Atlantic. From the ground, it's a montage of wrought iron gates, stone walls marbled with lichen, driveways that twist into a dream of trees. Beyond is fire and flood. The West has begun its long burn while rains soak the plains. The Mississippi surges. A climate group blocks traffic with a boat, pours blood on the streets of London. In Paris, a great cathedral stands charred.

In Nearwater, a boy walks through the trees, a recent arrival, a child of old wealth and breeding. There is only the sound of his feet treading the earth, the crunch of leaves and twigs, the same crunch made by deer and coyote, by the leather-shod feet of the earliest people. From time to time, he reaches for the phone in his back pocket and stops walking. He focuses the camera on something—a rodent skull, a tree that's fainted into the crook of another's branches—and takes a photograph.

He's no longer a boy, technically, but a man of eighteen, a free agent. He walks in the woods after work without purpose, and each day emerges to a new part of town. Today, he arrives at the Nearwater Country Club. The hollow pock of tennis balls, the lazy seesaw of birdcall. He comes to the edge of the tree line near the courts and there, on a boulder covered by a beach towel, is a girl. She's young—not yet a teenager—in a modest two-piece bathing suit, knees drawn up, lost in a book. Her hair hangs loose around her shoulders in damp ropes. The boy stands beside a tree, and as he watches, the girl turns a page of her book. He pulls the phone from his pocket and silences the camera shutter.

The girl looks up. Her eyes are wide and gray, her face pale and mournful as a saint's. Silently, he lowers the phone.

2.

INUTEMAN LANE RUNS a mile east of the tennis courts. The Rader house is set well back from the road, built to resemble a nautilus: cylindrical glass with white piping, windows ascending a spiral, reflecting a wide wreath of trees. Beach roses flank the door. The driveway is long and sinuous, an umbilical cord to the street. Strangers sometimes inch in to look; occasionally someone takes pictures. With the lights on at night, the furniture is visible from outside: the Roche Bobois dining chairs, the white couches and daybed. Inside, the entrance hall drops to a sunken living room, a round amphitheater with floor-to-ceiling windows. A small Jean Arp sculpture sits on a side table, insinuating the form of a woman. There's a Glas Italia console table, a Frank Gehry rock bowl. The edgier photographs—abstract macro studies of Louisa Rader's own body—were taken down when her daughter was born. An innocuous antique map of the galaxy now occupies their place.

Sylvie Rader sits eating a wedge of quiche at the kitchen island, balanced on a stool like another curated piece of art. She wears a sleeveless white shirt tucked into shorts that are too small. Her mother has bought her training bras, but she doesn't wear them, and her budding nipples are discernible through the shirt's fabric. Her bare legs hang down from the stool, long, skinny, and scabbed from insect bites. Next to her plate is a wadded paper napkin where she's wrapped the fatty chunks of ham she won't eat, their juices seeping through to the countertop. Beside the napkin is her new phone, an end-of-sixth-grade gift. It rests facedown, reflecting light off its polished case.

Upstairs, Louisa stands at the walk-in closet organized by season: tennis skirts at one end, fur and cashmere at the other. Tonight, she chooses a backless Dior dress she'd once worn for a fashion shoot and was allowed to keep—the kind of black dress that as a girl she hoped she might wear as a woman. She seizes a pair of closed Louboutin pumps despite the summer heat. When the doorbell chimes, she clips downstairs to open the door for the babysitter. It's Rosalie Warren's older girl, tramped up in a crop top and high-waisted jean shorts like the ones Louisa wore in the nineties. Her liquid eyeliner is deftly applied, the lower half of her hair uniformly bleached. This is a look shared by many of the town's teenagers, Louisa has noticed, likely achieved through hours of video tutorials.

"Hi," Sylvie says to the babysitter, then looks back dolefully into her bowl. Doleful. This is the word that sometimes comes to mind when Louisa thinks of her daughter.

Sylvie had been adamantly opposed to having Rachel come. To be fair, most girls Sylvie's age already stay home alone, and the babysitter is only a few years older than she is. But Richard dislikes the thought of leaving their daughter for even a few hours. He's a worrier by nature and fatherhood has made him worse. The house has too many windows, he says. Even hiring a babysitter makes him nervous. Teenagers are dangerous with their inappropriate influences and their phones, which are fatal distractions. He's already proposed canceling tonight. No one will notice if they miss one party. But Louisa has held firm. Even though it's only a small event at Kelly Pratt's place, Louisa feels a minor rush at the mere idea of leaving home.

Entrusting their daughter to the babysitter in the glass house, they drive over the well-kept roads of Nearwater, roads named for colonial settlers, patriot soldiers, long-ago farm owners. An occasional gulf in the wall of trees offers a glimpse of an ancient graveyard, the mottled green stones of those first hearty settlers. Tucked between the taller stones are the smaller markers for the children and the flat blank rocks for the stillborns. Beneath all of these, the bones of the nameless indigenous.

The town has changed little since Louisa was a girl. Its summers are the same as they've been for a hundred years:

fireworks, gin, and golden retrievers. There's still just one commercial stretch where shop windows display Vera Bradley handbags, monogrammed children's clothing, and house listings. Through debate and decree, Nearwater has always prohibited chain restaurants and allows no neon—nothing beyond one modest sign on a neat storefront, no larger than two feet by four.

Perversely, Richard had been keen on settling here in particular. Louisa protested at first but had found no solid cause for refusal. Privately, she was somewhat relieved. It was comfortable and unchallenging to come back. She has few real connections to the place anymore, with her schoolmates scattered and her parents decamped to Hilton Head. Her childhood home has been so radically remodeled that only a buzz of memory persists at that address. Nearwater was an easy start, fresh and familiar at once. She knows how Richard detests the neighboring towns with their new construction too close to the road, showy monstrosities exposed to all eyes and traffic. Nearwater keeps its wealth relatively understated. He'd chosen a plot away from the center of town, without close neighbors. He'd submitted plans and received a permit immediately. The town was proud to gain the cachet of his name.

They park the Jaguar along the road and walk to the party address, which was once the home of a childhood friend of Louisa's, where she'd spent many happy afternoons. There'd been a badminton net and a great sledding hill. That friend and her parents have long since moved away, and now the house belongs to Kelly Pratt, a girl Louisa knew in high school who'd never quite left Nearwater.

Upon approach, Louisa is abashed that she spent any time choosing her clothing for the party, that she felt any excitement at all. In school, Kelly Pratt had been one of those girls no one noticed, one of the blush-toned clones Louisa assumed she'd leave far in her wake. They'd never been friends, and it's almost certain Kelly knows nothing of Louisa's time in New York. Unless, of course, she'd flipped through a magazine twenty years ago in her campus infirmary and found a photo spread. She might have seen Louisa reclined in a field of poppies, draped in Versace, a dragon stretching the length of her dress, spouting fire—this woman who'd once had a locker not eight feet from hers.

And yet now, here they are. As the door opens, Kelly's round face appears, carnation pink, matching her blouse. Her hair is still cut in the same bob with bangs. Louisa smiles reflexively, expansively, despite herself.

"Careful, someone just spilled a drink in the hallway," Kelly warns, kissing Louisa's cheek and then Richard's. "So glad you could come."

"So are we," Louisa says.

The inside of the house bustles, its air laden with perfume and the smell of baked canapés. Louisa is surprised to not recognize the first few people she sees bunched like magnets at the kitchen threshold.

7

"Everyone's out back," says Kelly. "Come, let's get you drinks."

As she leads the way, Louisa's snap impression of the house is that it lacks charm or character. The hallway is hung with the requisite family portraits, the Pratts posed in matching white linen and khaki on the beach, blond and tousled. They pass the formal living room where two little girls sit tinkling at a piano. Richard glances at Louisa, who feigns innocence. The truth is that the party invitation hadn't specified either way about children. Louisa hadn't asked about bringing Sylvie because she preferred to leave her home. It's so rare to have a night out with other adults.

French doors stand open to the back terrace, which is already crowded with guests. Kelly Pratt vanishes into them, and Richard puts a hand to Louisa's bare back, guiding her toward the bar. She feels light. In truth she's happy to be here, surrounded by animated faces. The phenomenon never ceases to strike her, that gatherings like this happen, that the drive to congregate is so strongly wired into human nature. These people, like her, are glad to be anywhere outside their own houses, sipping cocktails.

Louisa surmises that all these sharp bristled haircuts are Greg Pratt's colleagues, all these men in pastel shirts with rolled-up sleeves. They each keep a hand in one chino pocket and grip a drink with the other, their wives beside them in tailored sheath dresses. All of their houses, she imagines, also contain family portraits on the beach.

Beyond the low fieldstone wall of the terrace, the lawn is as marvelous as Louisa remembers. A green expanse rolls sumptuously to a thick border of trees. Children careen on the grass.

Greg Pratt holds court near the bar, face already flushed. His stout torso is attached to his head by a pleated walrus neck, but he still has all his hair and a surfeit of energy, which he spends on golf and bond trading. The "cultural" side of things, as he's saying now, comes from Kelly, whose directives Greg obeys without question. He tells his guests how he'd been game to vacation in Peru, to buy local crafts and eat exotic food. Now he stands with his gin by the bar, howling so loudly about it that the chuckling group around him stands several feet back. He catches sight of Louisa and Richard and booms, "Richard Rader, get a drink and get over here!"

"White wine, please," Louisa tells the bartender, an awkward college student.

"Same for me," Richard says.

The boy behind the pop-up bar pours the wine slowly and hands the first glass to Louisa with exaggerated grace.

Greg continues telling stories about Peru, gesturing with the tumbler in his hand. Louisa can see that Richard isn't listening. He's watching the children roll down the hill. A mother climbs over the wall and scoops her daughter up under the arms. The girl's yellow dress is streaked with grass stains.

"There were freakin' llamas everywhere!" roars Greg, and his audience laughs.

Louisa watches a black-haired girl try to do a succession of somersaults down the hill, falling sideways into a logroll. Another girl follows, somersaulting only once before her limbs shoot out like a starfish. She tries to cling to the ground but skids and tumbles. When she finally comes to a halt, she lies still for a moment, then begins wailing. No mother arrives to help, and the girl eventually calms herself and stands.

Greg shifts eye contact from person to person as he narrates.

"*'You call that a waterfall?'* I said to the guy. It was more like a leaky faucet, just a couple of rocks and a pond. Anyway, there we are standing there pretending to admire everything, and all of a sudden my pack llama tries to sit down right in a puddle. I could see her knees starting to bend, so I just started pounding on her and yelling, '*Get the hell up!*' And I guess she understands English, 'cause she did."

Richard laughs good-naturedly with the rest of the group.

Greg turns to him. "Hey, Richard, didn't you design a llama barn for Roy Fox?"

Richard smiles. "No, it was for camels." He takes an ironical sip from his wineglass. Although Louisa sometimes wishes he were more scintillating company, she's glad he's nothing like Greg. She excuses herself and edges her way out of the circle. She knows Richard won't follow.

Louisa looks down the hill to the place where the trees bleed together like ink. The impulse to roll toward them, to roll far away, is strong. The sky has begun to darken to a rich blue dome. Louisa feels a mild pang for Sylvie.

As she observes the fresh young couples, her eye belatedly catches on the faces of Steve and Lane Ramsey. She instinctively takes a step back, swivels away. To her shame, a shot of adrenaline goes through her as if she's come upon a menace. She makes herself take a deep breath. It seems wrong that these two should be out socializing after all that's happened. They have an aura now, a dangerous fame. It's impossible, for those who know, not to associate them with tragic contagion. Still, the right thing to do is dig up the courage and approach with a smile, touch Lane on the shoulder the way she might with anyone else at a party. But this courage is unavailable to Louisa. Maybe it's better to refrain, better to let the Ramseys find new people who can smile and chat with them in cheerful ignorance. No one can blame the old ones from shrinking away.

Louisa searches for a safe place to stand. Richard is nowhere to be seen on the crowded patio. Off to the side, beyond the fieldstone perimeter, there's nothing but emerald grass. No one has ventured there except for one person. To Louisa, he appears only as a long-limbed figure lying on the ground, arms folded over chest, legs thrust outward. Just an impression, a still image within the swirling bazaar.

Something in the figure's attitude suggests to Louisa the imperious manner of youth.

She goes through the rest of the crowd slowly, maintaining an abstract smile. It occurs to her that she could have brought her camera. She could have withdrawn to the sidelines, maybe, and made these partygoers her subjects. She could have framed the details that told the story, the way she used to do in the city. With a zoom lens, she might have pulled it off without notice. The crease of a dress hem, the stray wisp of a topknot. Suddenly, a thick pink arm curls around her waist.

"Have you met the Von Maurens?" Kelly asks. Louisa begins to reply that yes, she knows them, but Kelly rattles on. "He's from Lichtenstein, very interesting, and she's just lovely. Their son's in preschool with Merritt. I'll introduce you later. Come inside for the slideshow." Kelly squeezes like a boa constrictor, pulling Louisa with her.

In the corner of her eye, the figure on the grass lies still. Now that the first charge of mingling has diminished, Louisa envies the boy's position beyond the flux of the party. She suppresses the desire to go sit there herself. This is a freedom only boys are permitted, not wives.

She endures the Andean slideshow, making astonished noises for Kelly and draining her third glass of wine. After the lights come on, she echoes the other women who vow on the spot to visit Peru.

At last, Richard finds her in the house and gently takes her by the elbow. They need to get back for the babysitter, he says loudly enough for the other women to hear. Louisa smiles in apology and gives Kelly Pratt an air-kiss. As they head toward the door, a couple intercepts them. The man is tall and elegant in a tie and jacket too warm for summer. The woman wears a tweedy skirt suit, also heavy for the season. Her hair is up in a simple sweep. She reminds Louisa of a queen on a coin.

"Heinrich, Agatha, how nice to see you."

Hearing these names, Louisa pulls out her most brilliant, camera-ready smile.

"This is my wife, Louisa. Louisa, this is Heinrich and Agatha Steiger."

"What an absolute pleasure to meet you both."

"The pleasure is ours," Heinrich says, holding her hand and bowing slightly, as if he might raise it to his lips. He has a face she instantly likes, broad and laugh lined, with spirited brown eyes behind glasses.

"How do you know the Pratts?" Richard asks.

"Greg is a colleague," Heinrich says. "They were kind enough to invite us. We don't get out much I'm afraid."

"Are you in town all summer?" Richard asks.

"Yes, all summer," Agatha answers. "Our son is working at the Fox property, so we are staying home. I don't think you've ever met Gabriel? He's here, though I'm not sure where." Agatha looks over her shoulder.

"There," Heinrich says, pointing to the figure on the lawn. "I'll get him."

13

"No, that's all right," Richard says. "We'll meet him next time."

Heinrich looks at Louisa and back at Richard. "My apologies, you were just on your way out. I hope we might invite you to the house sometime? Please come for dinner."

"That would be wonderful," Richard says.

Louisa pushes even more wattage into her smile. "We'd love that, thank you."

They discuss the Steigers on the way home. Louisa has heard so much about the commission, one of Richard's biggest. The house was just finished a few months ago, and he's thrilled with it. He'd loved working with them, a cut above his usual clientele. They're from Austria, old nobility. They came to the States for Heinrich's business, some legacy of banking. They're art collectors, important in Europe, and philanthropists here. Heinrich has a defunct noble title, but Richard can't remember what it is.

"They seemed lovely," Louisa says in the car. She still feels a spangle over her skin as if she's received a sacrament. "You can tell, just looking at them, that they're a different class."

Richard nods. "Yes, they are."

Back home, Louisa removes her Louboutins and climbs the stairs. She feels the loose-jointed disorientation of returning from a party, floaters drifting in her vision. The silken fabric of her dress is an exquisite pleasure, sliding over her bare thighs with each step. The party was satisfying. The very end, meeting the Steigers had shifted it from triviality to significance. What, exactly, is this significance? She probes the feeling. They're wealthy and powerful, yes, but what does she expect from them? Does she think they'll breathlessly discover and patronize her own neglected artwork? Does she want them to donate to Nearwater's provincial art center? Or does her excitement stem simply from brushing against clout?

At the top of the stairs, Sylvie's bedroom door is ajar. Through the slit, Louisa can see her daughter's head resting on the pillow like a dark moth. Her phone is on the nightstand beside her; Louisa had forgotten to tell the babysitter their rule against this. Horse show rosettes adorn the wall near the bed, ordered by color. Yellow third-place ribbons ruffle the wall over Sylvie's head like small golden suns. Again, Louisa has a pang of regret for not bringing Sylvie to the party. She remembers the old routine of reading aloud before bed every night. Sylvie had valued the time with her mother, holding her hand as she read, asking what words meant, begging for just one more page, one more sentence. Louisa hadn't acceded often enough, she thinks now. She should have extended bedtime, soaked up all the love she could. At some point the routine had faltered and ceased altogether.

Louisa withdraws to the master bedroom, where she undresses and runs a bath. For distraction, she takes an issue of *ARTnews* into the tub, letting its pages warp. It feels a little dangerous to surrender to very hot water, to feel her pulse slow, see her limbs float. Her brain, robbed of elasticity, makes little sense of the paragraphs of text. She skips over the profiles and reviews and just surveys ads for upcoming shows. A bright square catches her eye, a floor carpeted with red balls. She stiffens at the name printed beneath. "New work by Angelica Ulmstead." Unbelievable. She comes back to Louisa like a ghost: the spiky red hair, the rubber-red lips, the absurd cigarette holder. Angelica even slept, they used to say, with a masturbating self-portrait over the bed. Now her show is about to open at Bernard Stirling's new Tribeca location.

Louisa turns the page with a slap to a feature on new minimalism, a full page devoted to one painting, a flat expanse of blue. The painting's effect is deficiently calming. A film has begun to form on the surface of the bathwater, bringing an itch to her skin. The magazine pictures taunt her, the dozens of showcased artists. There's a full-length photograph of a young woman in a man's shirt and tie and paint-smeared jeans, staring dead-eyed into the camera, her canvases stacked behind her. These young ones don't consider the risk of failure; they believe intention leads to success. And so it has, here in these pages of *ARTnews*. Louisa stands up in the tub and wraps herself in a fresh white towel.

She goes downstairs in her bathrobe without a destination. There's the familiar crack of light under the door of Richard's office, but she doesn't want to speak to him now. She goes to the screened porch and stands, watching the slow hole of night open around her. A strict circumference of light bands the nearest grass. There appears, from this standpoint, no world beyond the black trees, nothing beyond this tight island. New York City seems a rumored place, an error of memory.

Louisa feels a gently persistent stab inside her ribs. She can't rid her mind of Angelica. It's been almost fifteen years since they last spoke, since she last saw Angelica or Xavier or anyone else from that life. Still, there's a dark pull, a question that tugs at her.

Her old Rolodex dwells in a sleek white cabinet. It's an artifact now with its own aura of history. She's never taken the time to copy the names and numbers into her phone, and so she takes the Rolodex outside to the lawn near the garage, out of view from the windows. She thumbs the yellowed card edges. It's late, but not too late for the city.

"Bernard," she says when he answers, her voice strange in the night. "It's Louisa Rader."

"Louisa, how the hell are you? Where are you?"

"Good, still in Connecticut. How are you?"

"Great, Louisa, I'm doing great. Well, how nice to hear from you."

"I just had the urge to say hello. It's been a long time."

"What a surprise."

There's an empty pause.

"I just saw the ad for Angelica's show." Louisa keeps her voice light. "I didn't realize she was still working."

"Ha. She's been working all this time it turns out. She disappeared for a while, you know, and then came back with some really interesting stuff. It kills me to have to show it during the summer, but she didn't want to wait. Really, it's fantastic work."

"Is that right," Louisa says.

"Well, you know, it's my kind of thing, anyway."

"I guess you're still not showing much photography."

"Not on the whole, really, no." Bernard pauses. "Very rarely."

Louisa attempts a forgiving murmur.

"Have you been working?" he asks after a moment. Just a courtesy.

"No, not lately. I'm busy with my daughter, and I think I told you I've been directing the art center in town."

"Right, right. That all sounds good, Louisa." Bernard's voice is earnest. "And, please, let me know if you need any help. I'm happy to introduce you to some new people."

"Thank you, I know you are."

She pauses and draws in the night air. The city bridges are so far from where she stands, blazing against the night sky. Louisa's heart works faster as she closes her eyes and waits, letting the moment pull taut before speaking again, forcing her voice out.

"Have you heard from Xavier recently?"

There's a beat of silence. "No. Not directly, anyway. He's been out of the loop for a while."

"I know he stopped working a few years ago."

"More than a few," Bernard goes on quickly. "He has no reason to call me. He has nothing to show. It's a shame."

"Yes, it is."

Bernard pauses again. She knows there's more.

"I don't think he's doing well," he says at last. "The last I heard, someone saw him sleeping in a doorway or something to that effect."

Louisa stands on the grass, feeling gnats at her ear. She waits for Bernard to continue. Insects circle in the flood-light above the garage, and all at once she remembers there might also be bats. They come out at dusk in summer and zag among the trees. If she were to look up now, she might see them above her.

She's one of the few who know that Xavier's real name is Peter, that he's from Kansas. She can barely envision his face now, only a sketch of sea-glass eyes and sharp jaw. She'd guessed, when his name stopped appearing in the magazines, what had finally happened. Bernard is wrong, though, about whether he's working. It's certain he's work-ing. He'll always be doing something, even sketching from his vantage on a threshold. No matter what, he's fiercely alive, a pulsing energy in the city. She can feel him there always.

"You should come down to Angelica's opening," Bernard says.

Louisa breathes out. "I'm not sure about that."

"Oh, but really." Bernard's voice is fatherly. "It's summer, it'll be quiet. Some of your old crowd will be there. Who knows, Xavier might even show up. And it would be lovely to see you."

"I'll think about it," Louisa says into the night.

She goes up to bed, though it's too early to sleep. They live like animals here, she thinks, taking shelter at dusk. She doesn't dare calculate the years since she last saw the sun rise from a rooftop. Each night carries her further away from that time.

As her eyes close, she hears Richard coming up the stairs. When he's home for any stretch, he has a routine. He reads in his office for an hour before coming to bed. There are gaps in his education he's determined to fill: religion and philosophy. Even though he has a bachelor's and a master's degree—even though he was the first in his Ohio family to attend college or maybe because of it—he feels that he'll never catch up. After graduation, he passed through New York like a stone through a tumbler. And as much as he loves Nearwater, Louisa knows the East Coast is still opaque to him. She knows that he intuits a code just out of reach, the ease of deep money. But beneath his alienation is a conviction of superiority. Richard is proud of his work ethic, his hand-wrought success. It seems to Louisa that he secretly looks down on their neighbors, the merely advantaged, for their unexamined complacence, their denial of life's complications. He's intellectually thirsty in a way they aren't. She loves this about him, even if she feels excluded at times—even if, at times, he seems to look down on her too.

Louisa keeps her eyes closed. She knows that he'll slide into bed with a preoccupied, distraught look on his face. The roil of his mind will be nearly audible as he rests on the pillow beside hers. He's full of convoluted thoughts, existential worry. Sometimes she wakes to find his eyes on her, watching from another place. Now, he comes into bed and lies stiff. She continues to imitate sleep.

In her mind, she goes back to the party. With regret, she remembers the Ramseys. It had been cowardly not to say hello. Their pain was so heavy, it would have been worth whatever discomfort it caused her to show a bit of human warmth. It hasn't even been two years since Katherine died. The school district where the Ramseys lived, adjacent to Nearwater's, had allowed a contractor to bury debris on school property in exchange for building a new sports field. An alarming number of students had fallen ill shortly afterward—Katherine, at twelve, with leukemia. When her hair fell out, several girls from the school shaved their own heads in solidarity. It was unsurprising that these girls approached the threat together, as a team. There's a mentality of sportsmanship in this area, a belief that no matter how tough the opposition, with enough verve and persistence the game can always be won. These are children raised by winning parents who've leapfrogged their way to the top or were born there. Disappointment and despair are foreign to this young generation, undefeated from birth.

Louisa is still haunted by their visit to the Ramseys'. She remembers the mailbox, satirically chipper, in the shape of a goose. She remembers the pink and violet hydrangeas that hugged the front of the house, the smell of the fresh-cut lawn as she and Sylvie approached the door. She'll never forget how Lane Ramsey looked when she opened that door: face gaunt, eyes stricken. She wore a peach tunic with jodhpur-style pants, and through her rack of white teeth she chirped, "Hello, girls, so nice to see you."

Louisa remembers the delicate vines on the wallpaper, the prettiest of prison bars. Katherine looked almost regal, propped in bed in her ruffled nightgown, surrounded by pillows and flowers, her ivory arms at rest on the bedspread. Her hair wasn't gone completely but clung in blond tufts. Louisa remembers the stuffed ducks and rabbits, the bookshelf with glass animals. It was the bedroom of a very young girl. Clustered on a bulletin board were horse show ribbons like Sylvie's. On the night table was a framed picture of Katherine on her favorite horse, Excalibur. The girls at the barn fed that horse extra carrots now, as if it were mourning too.

"I miss riding the most," Katherine said. "It's the first thing I'll do if I get better."

"You mean *when* you get better," Sylvie countered. She was ten years old then.

"Well, I might not," Katherine said.

Louisa wanted to interject here, to change the course of the conversation, keep it light and safe. But there was something in the girl's face that stopped her.

"I'm not afraid, though," Katherine continued. "I've thought a lot about it, and I realize that I don't have to be afraid. We weren't afraid to be *born*, were we?"

Sylvie glanced down. "I don't know."

"Dying isn't anything, really. It's just going back to wherever we came from." Katherine's eyes were open wide, as if it were crucial that she convey this message. "I don't want anyone to be afraid for me, or sad."

Sylvie didn't respond. Louisa felt gigantic, towering over the girl in bed.

"Promise you won't be afraid or sad," Katherine said, with an insistence close to anger.

"Okay, I won't be," Sylvie murmured.

Katherine looked away. There was a long pause before she spoke again. "So, tell me about riding."

"We're doing three-foot jumps now," Sylvie said softly. There was a quaver in her voice as if she might cry, and in that moment Louisa ached for her.

"Really?"

"It's not so bad," Sylvie said, gathering herself. "But on Cracker it seems a lot higher."

After a beat, Katherine smiled. Her face was thinner to be sure but more elastic as well, as if every smile counted.

Her mother sat on the edge of the rocking chair, giving the stuffed animals space. Her face seemed strangely lit.

Louisa had felt a twinge of shame as she started the car engine. When they left, Lane Ramsey's day would continue, this new kind of hideous day. The tires crunched rudely over the gravel as Louisa backed out past the goose mailbox and onto the road. A few months later, the Raders were at the memorial service, watching the Ramseys come down the church aisle. There was a spray of pink flowers at Lane's breast. Steve held her elbow as if keeping her upright, and their son walked beside them, matching his steps to theirs. Katherine's friends, those shaved-head girls, linked arms and sang like monks. The song marked their release from Katherine. It was a song of joy for themselves, for growing their hair back, going to school, leaving the town and their families, making their own families, not dying young. At the cemetery, the first selectman gave a speech as a tree sapling was planted. The new tree would symbolize rebirth, he said.

After the service, Sylvie was more withdrawn than usual. She skipped meals and closed her bedroom door, and Richard was overcome with anxiety. He knew they shouldn't have let Sylvie visit Katherine when she was sick. He feared it had harmed her on some level. It was their job as parents to protect her from pain and fear, he insisted—and what was Katherine's death if not an impenetrable terror? Louisa argued that to shield a child from the truth was worse. It was their job as parents to equip her for the inescapable. He wanted to take Sylvie to therapy, but Louisa thought that would worsen the problem, give the episode the imprint of adult concern. Sylvie and Katherine hadn't really been close friends outside of riding. Kids were resilient, and they understood a lot more than parents gave them credit for. Sylvie would process this at her own pace, if they let her. She'd integrate it into her understanding of the world, which was, after all, deeply barbarous.

Still, though, as Louisa lies in bed, the image of Katherine's gravesite returns to her. She again sees the tree sapling as it looked standing alone, after everyone had gone. She sees it balanced in the mound of soil where it was planted, its thin limbs angled up like the reaching arms of a child. She remembers the unnatural aspect of it, stretching to the sky. It seemed the tree was frozen in this pose of wretched pleading, unable to bring its arms down.

3.

ON BLACK BROOK Road, the Steiger house crouches in the trees. Although Louisa has seen pictures, even visited the construction site, it's still a surprise that her husband has created this dark, private dwelling. It's so different from their own glass house. A shadowed inverse. The new residents seem to have added little—no flowering bushes near the doorway, no bright frame of welcome. They've cleared only as much land as needed for the structure to be raised. The rest is dense forest. They'd requested that the windows be scaled down so as not to advertise themselves, as they put it, to the outside. Only a few apertures betray the glow of inner rooms.

Approaching the door with Richard, Louisa feels the unease of a girl visiting her parents' friends. She touches the hem of her white suit jacket. Their daughter is between them in a dress of her own choosing, a secondhand wrap better suited to the beach, but Louisa hadn't wanted to argue. Sylvie has been boycotting new clothing, new anything. It has something to do with the environment, the dictate of *reduce, reuse, recycle*. Her brown hair is threaded with strands of copper, the ends perpetually stringy. Louisa wishes she'd made her brush it in the car. It irritates and worries her that Sylvie doesn't make the effort to groom herself. Her peers will shun her soon if they haven't already.

"So wonderful to see you," Agatha says, pecking each of Louisa's cheeks. "What a lovely daughter."

Sylvie flickers a smile.

"We're so glad you came," Heinrich says, taking Louisa's hand and kissing it.

The foyer is horizontally paneled in mahogany that reflects warm lamplight. It smolders with winter and secrecy. For a terrible moment, Louisa is unsure whether they should remove their shoes. But Heinrich and Agatha are wearing shoes, of course, and as they lead the way into the living room, Louisa realizes how ludicrous it would be for them to receive guests in stocking feet.

The living room is fully furnished as if it's been that way forever, the walls decked heavily with gilt-framed paintings.

"I can't believe you've done all this in, what, three months?" Louisa hears herself say in mock surprise, the default tone of polite adulthood.

"We were living in Nearwater already for a year, renting," Agatha says. "Just waiting for this house to be done. Our furniture fit in perfectly, and the art. We were at home right away."

The house already has an odor, woody and sweet. It reminds Louisa of a forested Austrian childhood she never had. She sits carefully on an antique settee with faded burgundy cushions and is struck by the incongruity of Richard's design—its signature angles and off-center doorways—with these furnishings of a European manor. Still, Louisa prefers this quiet elegance to the brassy displays of clients like the Foxes. Richard had designed an asymmetrical cedar addition for the Foxes' sprawling stone manse, as well as outbuildings in the same aesthetic vein to serve as shelters for their menagerie. That visit had been like stepping foot into Versailles or some Gilded Age pleasure garden. Even with its collection of extravagant creatures—everything from flamingos to lemurs—the estate seemed to suffer from a lack of imagination. It bristled with overindulgence, insecurity. The Raders had been lucky to visit, though, when Sylvie was small. The Foxes make few invitations anymore—not since the kindergarten field trip when a child was clawed by a wildcat. Sylvie had talked about the animals for weeks afterward. She'd especially loved the red pandas and, of course, the Bengal tiger.

Tonight's visit won't be nearly as exciting for her. Heinrich extracts a liquor bottle from a carved cabinet. "Dubonnet?" he offers. Agatha gives a crystal glass of ginger ale to Sylvie, who droops in an armchair while her father circumnavigates the room. Louisa feels like a young girl herself, sitting primly on the settee. Here, her height, usually a source of pride and power, seems to suggest American excess. She feels gawky, unsophisticated. She was slow to understand how important the Steigers are in the international art world, even after Richard told her about the Kunsthaus Steiger in Vienna, stocked with their private collection. Their tastes range from Renaissance to modern, and the Kunsthaus holds everything from Dürer to Klimt. They own a few tamer Schieles, and a new wing features a foray into more contemporary works, although nothing transgressive: Lucian Freud, Neo Rauch, some photorealist Richters. In this room, too, there's a mix of old and somewhat less old, all unsurprising. Each painting is illuminated by a hooded lamp.

As Richard approaches a painting, Heinrich offers, "This is a Rottmann. A nineteenth-century romantic, favorite of King Ludwig of Bavaria. One of my favorites, too, and quite rare."

The name of the artist is unfamiliar to Louisa. She sips her aperitif and smiles at Agatha. Sylvie pages through a coffee table book, written in German.

"That's a pretty good book, no?" Agatha asks with a wink, and Sylvie closes it. Her glass of ginger ale rests on the wooden table.

"Sylvie, use a coaster please," says Louisa, although she sees none.

Agatha purses her lips and fans her hand as if waving the idea away. Sylvie leaves the glass where it is.

The men move to the next painting, a portrait of a noble-woman in rubies. Louisa has little patience for the history of trite art. These are exceptional pieces to be sure, in terms of scarcity, but aesthetically not much different than the minor Hudson River school paintings her parents had once hung on their own Nearwater walls. This careful class of people, no matter how wealthy, always seems to welcome daring architecture before daring art.

Agatha turns to Louisa.

"You run the art center in town I hear?"

"Yes," Louisa answers. "I curate the exhibitions."

Louisa hears Heinrich's oaky voice explaining that the woman in the portrait is a relative of some kind. She resists asking whether she's a countess, whether Heinrich is techni-cally a count. Or a baron. She isn't clear on the difference.

"It's a beautiful art center," says Agatha.

"I agree," Louisa answers. "Richard designed the expan-sion, you know. It used to just be an old carriage house. He kept the historic façade, but the gallery and studios are all new. And the audio building."

"No one ever uses that, though," Richard interjects.

"Not yet, but we will," Louisa says, smiling. "It's my favorite part of the center I think. Just gorgeous, like a jewel box in the woods. Completely black inside with soundproof walls and a retractable ceiling."

"It would make a great observatory," Richard adds wryly. "Some night we'll take Sylvie there with a telescope."

"He really is very talented," Agatha says. "We're so happy to have found him."

Louisa smiles. The men shift to another painting.

"This one is Achenbach," she hears Heinrich say. "Unusual to see a genre scene like this from him."

Agatha stands. "Sylvie, this must not be very interesting for you. Would you like to go to the TV room?"

Sylvie rises and skulks after her. When Agatha returns to her seat, she faces Louisa with a new freshness. "How long have you lived in Nearwater?" she asks.

"I grew up here, actually," Louisa tells her. "It's been twelve years since we came back."

"I understand why you would," Agatha says. "It's a lovely town. I wish we'd found it sooner."

Louisa nods, feeling unaccountably restless, and rises to her feet before she can acknowledge the impulse to stand. A row of framed photographs on the mantel gives her a destination, and she steps toward them under the pretense of getting a closer look at the painting above.

"This one's lovely," she says, pretending to study the landscape. A man leads a horse near the bank of a river, both figures expressed with a few touches of paint.

"That's another Rottmann," Heinrich offers. "Not as large as his more important works but just as painstakingly done."

"Yes, even the horse," Louisa says, then drops her eyes to a photograph on the mantel. A handsome boy sits in a patch of sunlight with a drawing pad. He looks up at the camera, a black slice of hair past one eye, light skin in stark contrast. The other eye is caught in the sun, a startling blue.

"Is this your son?" Louisa asks, lifting the picture.

"Yes," Agatha answers. "That's Gabriel."

"Where *is* Gabriel?" Heinrich asks his wife. "He said he'd come up to say hello."

"Oh, there's no need for that," Louisa says, putting the frame back on the mantel.

"Is he your only child?" Richard asks.

"Yes," says Agatha.

"Sylvie's our only too."

"Well, you're very lucky. She seems like a very sweet girl. How old is she?"

"She turned twelve in April," Louisa says. "And Gabriel? He looks to be about the same age."

"That's an old picture. He's eighteen. Nineteen this fall."

"Oh, is he home from college?"

"No," says Agatha. Louisa waits for more, but Agatha offers nothing else.

There's no music. Only their four voices fill the room. Louisa looks at Agatha with a smile meant to represent goodwill and gratitude. She takes another sip of her aperitif, which is almost gone now. She's begun to feel a warm radiance from the liquor, an intensification of the sense memory she had upon entering the house, the woodland familiarity. It suggests an intimacy with the Steigers. There's something different about them, beyond the fact that they're foreign, an

33

implacable serenity that both attracts Louisa and unsettles her. They seem deeply comfortable with themselves and each other. Composed, genteel, kind.

They discuss Nearwater and its neighboring towns. The most prestigious, there's no need to mention, is their own.

"Louisa grew up here, actually," Richard says with a note of pride, putting a hand on her shoulder.

Agatha smiles at her with warm, assessing eyes. "Yes, she mentioned that."

"Nearwater's a great investment," says Richard. "And the taxes pay off with the school system."

Agatha and Heinrich smile thinly. Louisa shoots a look at her husband, who remains oblivious. At that moment a young man enters the room. He comes toward them with fluid movements, and Louisa puts her glass down. She's struck by his height and posture. Although he wears ripped jeans and a loose black T-shirt, there's something authoritative in his bearing.

"I'm Gabriel," the young man says.

Louisa stands to shake his hand and feels that she's touched a socket. She pulls away quickly. She watches him grip her husband's hand, quick and firm, and deliver an easy smile.

"It's a pleasure to meet you both," he says.

Back downstairs in his basement studio, the boy clips a piece of drawing paper to an easel. He holds a pencil to the paper and closes his eyes for a minute. He begins to sketch a female figure, tall and thin as a drinking straw in a slim white suit, hair a black sheet cut at the chin.

As he works, the sound of footsteps comes from the basement stairs. He turns and looks. When he glances up, his eyes meet the eyes of the girl from the tennis courts. She stops on the stairs.

"Hi," the boy says.

"Hi."

"It's okay," he says. "You can come down."

"Sorry. I just heard someone down here and was curious."

The boy smiles. "Don't apologize for being curious."

The girl descends the remaining steps and looks questioningly at him. "Didn't I see you in the woods the other day?"

"Yes, that was me. I didn't mean to scare you."

"You didn't."

"I was just taking a walk," he says.

"Okay."

They're both quiet for a minute.

"This is my house," the boy says. "It seems your father designed it."

"He did," says the girl. "He designed our house too."

The boy looks back at his drawing paper. The girl studies his face in profile. It's the face of a boy but also a man, with dark brows, curved lips, an Adam's apple at the throat.

"Do you go to the high school?" she asks.

"No."

"Oh, did you graduate?"

"I left." The boy looks at her and smiles. His smile is soft, his eyes full of light and play.

"You left?" the girl asks. "Do you mean you dropped out?"

"Technically I was expelled. But I like to think of it as a strike on school."

The word "expelled" lingers in the air. The girl smiles uncertainly. "So, now what? Are your parents teaching you or something?"

"No, I'm teaching myself."

She nods, as if in understanding.

"I always hated school. Don't you?" he says. "I hated the teachers who took my drawings away and said, 'It's not drawing time, it's learning time.'"

"Me too," she says. She looks around at the clutter of easels, piles of books, cans of solvents, palettes. "Are you an artist?" She sits on the edge of a fold-up cot strewn with bedsheets.

The boy looks at her scabbed legs. "Yeah," he says. "This is my studio."

The air is heady with vapors of paint and turpentine. Ceiling lights point at the drawing easel and in every other direction. There's everything an artist could want but barely enough room to turn around. It's several degrees cooler than the rest of the house, like the hull of a ship.

The girl gets up and circles the room. Her eyes linger on a deer skull. She leans in to inspect an iridescent green beetle, carved from rubber. Then she looks at the high window ledge, but she's too short to reach the animal figurines that are lined up there.

"That's the ark from the flood myth," the boy tells her. "I've been carving them for years. Which one do you like best?"

After a moment, she points to the tigers, and he brings one down for her. Each stripe is carefully painted, each whisker, and the downturned disapproving mouth.

"That's my favorite, too. You can have it."

She looks at it carefully, turns it over in her hand. "Thanks. Did you seriously make all these?"

He smiles. "I'll show you how sometime, if you want."

"Why are you making Noah's ark? Are you religious?"

"Yes and no. This one's a new ark for our time. Climate change, melting glaciers, all the coming floods."

"They're really good."

For a moment, the girl stands in the glare of the ceiling lights, surveying the studio, the jars of crusted paintbrushes. Her eyes land on the easel where the boy has begun to outline the woman.

"Who's that?" she asks.

"Oh, it's just a sketch I started. From my imagination."

She glances at him.

"You should go back up to your parents."

"Can I see your drawing when it's done?" she asks.

"Sure," he says. "I'll send you a picture. Give me your info."

After she's gone, he finds a long hair in a lazy spiral on the cot.

Upstairs, Heinrich refills Richard's glass and his own. He leans back in a damask chair and crosses one leg over the other, comfortable with the pause in conversation. Louisa has resumed her place on the settee.

"How did you begin collecting?" Richard asks. His voice is reedy compared to Heinrich's.

"I've been collecting my whole life. Many of these paintings were inherited from my father and some from his father before him. Really, the art has been in the family for generations, but I'm afraid I've been a bit too ardent in adding to it. The Kunsthaus has given us somewhere to put things, but this has only encouraged my problem."

"Well, are you ready for the grand tour? Not that you need it," Agatha says to Richard.

"Oh no, you're wrong. I hardly recognize the house." Richard pauses. "What I mean is that you've made it your own, and I'm glad to see that."

Heinrich leads the group through the house, then up the stairs to the second floor. The last door opens to the master bedroom, which contains a large canopy bed and an antique boudoir. Louisa glimpses a speckled mirror, a row of pewter hairbrushes, a black-and-white wedding photograph in a silver frame. From a distance, Louisa can discern Agatha's ornately laced dress and Heinrich's tight jacket, its sash and medals.

They return to the living room for another round of Dubonnet. The conversation focuses on the details of the Steigers' house, and Richard launches into a long-winded explanation of his decision to place the staircase in the rear. It has to do with the poetics of negative space, of nurturing the role of absence. The concept of the qualitative leap. His voice rises another register as it gains enthusiasm, and he puts down his glass in order to use both hands in illustrating his points. Louisa looks at her watch and excuses herself to check on Sylvie.

She follows the sound of the television but finds the room empty. Louisa waits for Sylvie to return from wherever she's gone. When after several moments she still hasn't appeared, Louisa checks the first-floor bathroom and finds it unoccupied. She feels a tightening knot of annoyance as she steps through the hall, listening. She pauses at the stairway before climbing softly to the second floor. A door stands ajar to one of the rooms they hadn't visited on the tour, and Louisa stops here. She says Sylvie's name quietly, then takes a step inside. She's immediately confronted by a large painting on the far wall over a bed. In the painting, animals stand near a body of water. Each creature is rendered in what appears to be a purposefully primitive style. A long-torsoed lion, a bull with an oversize head, and a standing bird with extended wings. A fourth creature appears to be part animal, part human. Louisa steps closer and sees that each of the animals is patterned with eyes.

Louisa surveys the rest of the room. The door to the closet is open, revealing a crush of clothing and shoes. Rough canvases lean together, messily stapled to their stretchers, all facing the wall. She instinctively goes to them and pulls the first one toward her. She peers at it upside down. A study of the bull from the larger painting. She goes through the others: all versions of the primitive animals, patterned with hard jet eyes. They're stunning and unsettling, painted with brash confidence.

She turns in a circle. There are no posters of athletes or women. There are only a few reproductions of paintings taped to the wall, which look as if they've been torn from books. Some images are blocks of kaleidoscopic color. Others are Renaissance era: Bosch's *Garden of Earthly Delights*, Piero di Cosimo's *Forest Fire*. She studies the lions, pigs, and deer running from flames, their tongues hanging, some with the faces of humans. The bed is unmade. A crumpled bedspread reveals red sheets. Impulsively, she touches the pillow, then leans down and puts her face to it. A faint, oily smell.

Louisa steps back from the bed, feeling an erratic pulse through her body. It's an insane risk to keep standing there. She pulls away, and as she descends the stairs finally hears Sylvie's voice among the others.

"There she is," Richard says as Louisa enters the living room.

She smiles, and the Steigers smile back. Everything is fine. They go into the dining room to a splendidly set table and sit for dinner.

Back outside, it's night, a full moon above. Richard starts the car, turns on the headlights, then switches the ignition off again and gets out.

"One minute. I just want to peek at the back of the house before we go." He walks around to the side and disappears into the trees.

Alone in the car, Louisa and Sylvie sit quietly. Finally, Louisa speaks without turning around.

"Sylvie, where were you before? I looked for you in the TV room and you weren't there."

Sylvie pauses before answering. "Downstairs."

"Downstairs where?"

"In the basement."

"You went in the basement by yourself? Sylvie, you know better than to do that without permission."

Sylvie is silent for a moment. "Gabriel invited me," she said.

"Gabriel?"

"He asked me to come see his studio."

"In the basement?"

"It's where he paints and stuff. He showed me some of his artwork."

Through the windshield, Louisa sees Richard emerge from behind the house. He walks toward the car.

Louisa swivels to look at her daughter's face, which is turned to the window, washed by the moon.

"Just as I thought," Richard says, opening the car door. "They said they'd trim the woods back, but they still haven't done it. The trees are obstructing the house."

They pull out of the driveway and go toward home. There's no sound from the back seat. Richard glances into the rearview mirror. "Are you tired, honey?" he says to Sylvie.

She doesn't answer.

"What's wrong? You okay?"

"I'm fine."

Richard looks at Louisa. She breaks away from his gaze and lets her eyes close for a moment. There was a time when Sylvie would have told her exactly what happened, but lately she's become secretive, defensive. This is typical for her age. Other mothers complain about it, too, and Louisa knows it would be fruitless to pry. Growing up is a slow withdrawal, and they have to let it happen, as much as it might hurt. She's always telling Richard this.

"Honey, are you sure?" Richard says to the mirror.

"I said I'm fine," Sylvie answers firmly.

Louisa opens her eyes and stares ahead as Richard drives. The town is strange in the moonlight, the houses set back from the road with steady lamplight at their windows, each a vessel in its own green sea.

4.

Daylight breaks on the horse show field at the Nearwater Hunt Club, adjacent to the country club. Louisa thinks it's absurd that shows begin so early. There are just a few cars in the lot, misted with dew. The only sound is the trilling of hidden birds.

Inside the barn, among muffled huffs and stamping hooves, Louisa watches Sylvie tack up her horse. She's been assigned Cracker today, which makes Louisa glad. Cracker is a safe horse the color of wheat. Sylvie has long had a touching affection for him, speaking softly into his ear the way girls do in books. Now, she digs out the grooves of his hooves, letting clumps of packed dirt and dung break apart on the floor. Her quiet focus is uncannily adult. Her riding instructor approaches, leading a palomino with a serrated row of braids along its neck.

"Hey, Sylvie, ready to rock?"

Curtis wears his own hair in layers that make it doubly lush. His jeans are always a bit tight at the crotch. Louisa notices that Sylvie blushes in his presence.

"Ready," Sylvie answers.

Curtis winks at Louisa, then continues on with the palomino.

For a stretch of weeks at the beginning of her riding lessons, years ago, Sylvie had come home somber and silent. It had taken days of questioning to pull it out of her—that there'd been an instructor who was too tough, shaming her in front of the other girls. Sylvie cried when she finally admitted to being afraid of cantering. Her daughter's anguish became a terrible pit in Louisa's chest. The anger she'd felt for that instructor had been deep and unprecedented. She'd lain awake that night and confronted the instructor the following day with measured words and a barely controlled urge to strike her. When a child is threatened, a mother rears up. It's the most natural thing in the world.

Louisa's gaze ventures down the aisle to where Katherine Ramsey should be getting ready for today's competition too. She and Sylvie should be together, comparing strategies like little men. Louisa thinks of the heavy anger Katherine's mother must be carrying. For Lane Ramsey, there's no instructor to confront, no one to strike.

Sylvie—naturally, wondrously—is still here. At the time of Katherine's illness, she came to Louisa one night. She said she was afraid she had cancer and was going to die. She couldn't explain why she thought this; it was just a feeling, a premonition. Louisa had comforted her, held her close, stroked her hair. They were quiet together, mother and baby.

Louisa whispered that everything was okay, the same phrase over and over, as she'd done when Sylvie was small. Then, together, they'd looked up the medical definition of cancer. They'd viewed the illustrations showing magnified pictures of cells—one set healthy, one set out of control. That was all there was to the disease, after all. The normal cells were tidy, their nuclei tight black pinpricks. The malignant cells were floppy and blurred, one melting into the next like bleeding egg yolks. Looking at them, Louisa felt a visceral horror.

"You don't have to worry, sweetie," she'd said to her daughter. "Almost all children have normal cells and are perfectly healthy. Most people who get cancer are old. Katherine's case is very, very rare. Also, if you had cancer, you'd feel sick. As long as you're feeling well, you're perfectly fine."

"But what if there's toxic stuff under the ground here too? What if it's in our water or food, poisoning us? How do we know it isn't?"

Louisa was silent. The disaster at Katherine's school was just a few miles away, in a town as comfortable as their own. Lawsuits were being filed by the victims, but it was unclear how amends would or could be made. As far as Louisa knew, no such construction debris had been buried in Nearwater, but this was just one threat of many. The truth was that there was danger everywhere. Everyone swam in the waters of trade-off: risk subsumed by profit. She thought of the plastic bottle Sylvie took to school each day, the rubberized straws and nipples she'd been sucking since she was an infant. She thought of the processed snacks, the sunscreen and insect repellents with benzene, all manner of chemicals impossible to avoid. She'd put a hand to Sylvie's back and rubbed gently.

"Maybe we should talk to Dr. Sharma about your worries. She'll be able to answer all these questions and make you feel better."

They had, in fact, visited the pediatrician, whose soothing voice and colorful wristwatch had placated Sylvie since toddlerhood. Sylvie listened and nodded as Dr. Sharma spoke. *Any other questions? Anything you'd like to ask without Mom here?* The doctor glanced sympathetically at Louisa. *No,* Sylvie said.

Now, Sylvie stands taller in her jodhpurs and show jacket. The jacket's tailoring flatters the new curve of her hips. She holds the reins like a young duchess while a groom works on Cracker, wiping out his nostrils and crouching to paint dark polish on his hooves. Neither Sylvie nor the groom seems to question their roles. When the horse is ready, Sylvie leads him out of the barn, Louisa walking alongside. Sylvie seems more taciturn than usual this morning. Looking at her daughter's face in solemn profile, Louisa is reminded of their night at the Steigers'. The disquiet from that night rushes back, and she feels a gut certainty that Sylvie is guarding something. Before she can think about it, the words are out.

"Did you have a good time at the Steigers' house the other night?"

As soon as she's spoken, she regrets it. Sylvie's face tenses. This, Louisa understands, is the absolute worst time to begin the conversation. If there's one lesson she's learned as a parent, it's that timing is everything. It's crucial to wait for the teachable moment, the reachable moment, the moment of supple receptiveness, as few and far between as they may be. It's a lesson she too often forgets.

"It was okay," Sylvie mutters.

They arrive at the warm-up ring where at least ten ponies canter in circles, piloted by young girls who somehow negotiate the same eight jumps without colliding.

Sylvie bends to tighten her bootlaces. Louisa wavers.

"So, you met Gabriel? What did you think of him? Was he nice?"

"Yes."

"What did you talk about?"

Sylvie straightens back up. Another girl enters the ring on a prancing black pony.

"I don't know. Nothing, really. He just showed me the basement."

"He paints there?"

"Yeah."

"Why didn't he come up for dinner?"

"He didn't feel like joining, I guess."

Louisa takes a slow breath. "Next time please ask before exploring someone else's house."

Sylvie doesn't respond. Louisa sees her jaw clench.

"Do you understand?"

"Yes."

"Okay. I just want you to understand."

Sylvie nods and is quiet again. Louisa, however ham-handedly, has done her job. Her worry dissipates as she watches Sylvie mount her horse and gather the reins. Cracker obeys whatever silent shift in weight tells him to move forward. It's a continual wonder to Louisa how poised her daughter is on horseback. She balances miraculously, convincing the horse that she's part of its body, and when they move together smoothly they become a mythical being, a centaur.

Louisa has never been on a horse; she's never had the desire. But she enjoys watching her daughter ride and is drawn to the spectacle of a horse show. It's pleasant to join the other mothers in the tent beside the show ring where they sit with their sun hats, Jack Russell terriers, and chilled rosé. This is equestrianism, sport of nobility, and this particular show is the glamorous apex of summer in Nearwater.

Today, Louisa has brought her camera and zoom lens. The grand prix tent is just beyond the pony ring, which gives her cover. Surreptitiously, she focuses the camera on the side of a woman's face, the anonymous laugh lines and neck wrinkles, the diamond floret at the earlobe. She presses the shutter button three times. Next, she captures the woman's hand, her tennis bracelet and nail polish, and almost doesn't notice when Sylvie enters the pony ring. She almost misses the moment when Cracker hesitates before one of the jumps—an extended pause, gathering his strength to leap—before launching gracelessly over.

Louisa comes in to work late after the show. Saturdays are always hard, especially when Richard is away, and she doesn't apologize for this. Some might consider it unprofessional. Talk might circulate that she's not serious, that she's a trophy wife, that Richard has inflated the art center as a toy to keep her occupied. It's true that when the director position opened, he'd encouraged her to apply. But most of the candidates had only had administrative experience with stuffy nonprofits. Louisa was the only applicant with any credibility in the art world, any vision at all.

She hates the old entrance sign, made of wood planks that belong on a mountain trail. She's been planning to commission modern signage, something sleek to complement Richard's renovation and signal the kind of art she's trying to attract. Eventually, she'll install contemporary sculptures on either side of the drive, create a kind of art trail. Maybe she'll curate some sort of piece for the trees, which are old enough to tent the driveway. Some of these oaks must predate the carriage house's construction. They may have been here even before the farmland was staked out and plowed, when it was Wappinger ground.

"No messages," Deirdre announces as Louisa comes in. Her hair is a new shade of red, nearly purple.

"Nobody called back from Merriwether?"

"Sorry, no."

Louisa's office is small and spare. Deirdre brings in a stack of magazines, then returns to the reception desk where she spends the day staring at her phone. Louisa, on the other hand, goes tediously through pages of color and print. There's a Japanese artist showing at Nine Lives: prodigious pen drawings like intricate wallpaper. Louisa envisions the walls of the art center gallery covered in such painstaking pattern. It will be fall soon, time for this more serious work that might bring visitors up from the city—and it would be enriching for the town, too, to see work by a Japanese artist. She hasn't done enough this year to expand the center's repertoire. The board claims they want to evolve, to join the vanguard of the art world, but they consistently reject work they deem too provocative or political. They'd expressed initial interest in Louisa's proposal to show a young Bronx artist—photorealist portraits of victims of police brutality—but eventually backpedaled. She should have known that the people of Nearwater wouldn't want the portrait exhibition. They wouldn't be able to see what it had to do with them, wouldn't know why they were being confronted by these images. It's easier to adhere to the usual fare: student work, watercolors by seniors.

It took a while for her to understand that anxiety is what drives the board. They're concerned about the town's declining school enrollment and aging tax base. They see the purpose of the center as increasing Nearwater's desirability, something that might attract new residents who'll congratulate themselves for choosing a vibrant community. She finally understands that they want to look edgy without risk, without alienating the elder population or scaring young newcomers. She's learning how to thread this needle. It had been a feeble vindication when the board unanimously approved a show of painless bright abstracts by a Trinidadian artist.

Sometimes, despite herself, she envisions her own work on display. Behind the rows of shoes in her closet, her professional portfolios abut the wall. One contains her modeling pictures, the other her photography. She never looks at them. Richard may not even know they're there. She hopes Sylvie hasn't gone exploring and found them. They aren't pictures she wants her daughter to see—strangers on the street, men at parties, intimate studies of flesh—and she knows they'd be anathema to the board.

"Louisa Rader from Nearwater Art Center. In Connecticut. Yes, all right, well, please have him call me. Regarding Etsu Sakamoto."

She puts a mint in her mouth and sucks on it. It's too much effort to lift the phone from its cradle again. In any case, they rarely call back.

There's little else to do today. It's almost always just her and Deirdre, the summer intern whose only real duties are to open and close the center, answer visitors' questions, and refill the tray of complimentary cookies and lemonade. Although they seldom speak at length, Louisa likes to imagine she's an influence on Deirdre, and she feels oddly ashamed that Deirdre should witness some of the substandard artwork Louisa accepts for the center. At the moment, the juried show of local painters is on view, judged by the high school art teacher. The winner is a portrait of somebody's grandmother, the prize ribbon hanging like an ornament in the old woman's hair.

"Stay right there," says Deirdre, appearing in the doorway of Louisa's office. Louisa sees the camera at the same instant she hears the shutter close.

"It's new," Deirdre says, with a metal click from her tongue ring. She holds out the Canon, and Louisa sees herself frozen on the screen. Just a silhouette backlit by the window. Not a very good picture.

"You're a photographer?" Louisa asks.

Deirdre shrugs. "Just starting out."

Louisa thinks of sitting Deirdre down, giving her the basics, telling her which rules to obey and which to break. It's all right, she'd say, if her first compositions aren't good.

Deirdre would have to follow the same uphill path every artist took. Not everyone, she'd warn, reaches the top. But Deirdre has already retreated to her desk, where she sits with the camera, skimming through images. Louisa knows the girl would only listen politely anyway, then do what she wants. To someone like Deirdre, Louisa's advice would seem obsolete. There might be a retro glamour in the old kinds of pictures—the Arbuses and Mapplethorpes—but no one wants more pictures like that. Now that everyone is a photographer, now that the world is awash in images, there's little magic left in them. What pictures remain to be taken? Louisa knows she's a curmudgeon to have these thoughts, like the classical painters who hated the impressionists and the impressionists who hated the expressionists. She knows it's a mark of decline to feel scorn for the arrogant children who think they can overturn the history of art with one thumb.

Louisa would like to tell Deirdre that she was once a young upstart too. When Xavier first pushed her to show her photographs to Bernard—when she'd been roundly rejected—it had taken a while to recover. *Competent but derivative* was what Bernard had said, and when Louisa thought about it, when she really studied her pictures, she knew he was right. They were too pretty. She was too attached to a traditional idea of beauty, still trying to make things that were visually pleasing. Xavier, on the other hand, was always slashing and failing, ripping things up. Louisa was petrified of making a mistake, creating something ugly and hateful, but Xavier scolded her. "You have to be uncomfortable," he said. "If it's comfortable, it's not art." After that, she forced herself to see things as they were. She took unflattering pictures of people at parties, unflattering pictures of herself. After developing these, she ruined them on purpose, coating them with resin, molding a fleshy texture on the surface of the prints. Xavier was ecstatic. He brought them to Bernard himself, demanded they be included in the next group show alongside his own work. Bernard didn't show photography, but these were technically multimedia, so he made an exception.

At that opening, Angelica Ulmstead hadn't held back her contempt. "Nepotism only goes so far," she'd growled to Louisa's face. "You might be able to weasel your way in, but fakes and phonies always fall away. Only nerve and sweat survive."

The first review called Louisa's work promising. The second one used the word "predictable." The others didn't mention her at all. They effused over Xavier and Angelica, heirs to de Kooning and Hannah Wilke. Xavier told her to ignore the lukewarm reviews and embrace the positive one—or even better, not read them at all. What set real artists apart, he told her, was fire. That was what forged his own balls into steel. Of course, there were times of doubt and despondency, but you had to keep going. "Like Beckett. 'I can't go on. I'll go on.'" He'd taken her face in his hands. "You have to get pummeled and bruised and be lying on the floor half-dead and still be able to pick up an arm and give everyone the finger."

She'd nodded and kissed him and said, "I know you're right." But he was right about himself, not her. Some people were born artists, held that conviction deep inside. The world had always told Louisa otherwise. She was the art, not the artist. Her gift was for easy beauty and elegance. This was no small thing, as much as she took it for granted. So many envied her. So many girls would have killed for her modeling career. Women had made lives out of much less.

Xavier had suggested that they move together to a live-work space in Bushwick. She'd have her own real darkroom, and if she was going to commit to her art, that was what she needed. But she'd vacillated, reluctant to give up her apartment, uncertain about the warehouse neighborhood that was graffitied and unlit at night. She told him it might be better if she stayed in Manhattan. It might be better for their relationship, for her own independence. He hadn't pushed. Instead, he'd gotten her friend Keith Hill to share the space with him.

Still, she'd had reason to believe she was on the cusp of success, that the next breeze would send her flying over. She found a job running an experimental art space on Avenue A where she again exhibited her smeared party pictures and was written up in the *Village Voice*. But then everything came crashing down with Xavier, and by the time she emerged from that maelstrom—by the time she grabbed on to Richard and was safely beached—the cusp seemed to have moved beyond reach. The art space closed down. The new kids wore cropped shirts and bangles again. They wanted arcane video, aberrant wax models, ironic knitwork.

Louisa remembers Angelica's upcoming show, the swarm of red balls. It's amazing that Angelica has managed to stay abreast of the scene all these years. For the first time, Louisa feels like congratulating her. Maybe she'll go to the opening, say hello, take the temperature. She should make an effort to see some new art at least.

Louisa stands and glides past Deirdre's desk. She sees that an older couple has entered the gallery, arms linked as they move around the room. They stand in front of a canvas, a monochromatic spiral with plastic ants affixed to it. Louisa takes a breath and steps into the gallery. Part of her job is to make visitors feel welcome.

"I don't know what this is supposed to be," the man says loudly. He turns to Louisa and gestures to the ants. "Those aren't real I hope!"

"No." Louisa forces a smile.

This isn't even challenging artwork, just effort by a local hobbyist. In any case, she prefers vocal visitors like these to those who walk into the gallery as if into a clothing store, coolly and silently, ignoring her as they might a clerk. She wants to inform those kinds of visitors that she was born in this town herself and can smell them as the transplants they are.

The couple in the gallery stands back from the plastic-ant piece. "I like the regular paintings better," the woman says.

Louisa nods, sweetening her smile. They slowly finish their round of the gallery, stopping to look at each piece together, commenting and glancing back at her. Deirdre sits impassively behind her computer, tuning them out.

Just a few minutes after the couple leaves and Louisa has returned to her office, she hears another visitor enter the gallery. She comes back out to find a young man. When he turns toward her, his face is a cold blast. She recognizes the black hair, the ghost-pale eyes. He's taller than she remembers, with the broad shoulders of a man. She realizes that she's holding her breath, just as she'd done when she'd first met Xavier.

He comes around to the office door and stops. He holds out a hand to her, and she takes it. "Good to see you again."

"And you, Gabriel."

He smiles. "I'm wondering if you have a program?" His voice rings in the gallery. Deirdre looks up from her computer.

"A schedule of classes?"

"Sure," he says.

Up close, his mouth is slightly strange, the top lip fuller than the bottom, so that the fit seems a degree off. It's an endearing glitch in his otherwise refined appearance, a shadow of boyhood.

"This is a school and a gallery, too, right?" he asks.

"Right." Louisa's heartbeat spikes. This, she remembers, is the boy her daughter saw in the basement. She holds up a finger and turns away. She doesn't want him following her into her office. She doesn't want Deirdre listening.

She comes back into the gallery and hands him a booklet, dense with glossy paper. She remembers the paintings she'd seen in his room and wonders if there are any instructors good enough to teach him.

He leafs through the booklet. "There's a residency program?"

"Yes. Well, no. Not yet," she answers.

"I'm an artist," he says.

"I know," says Louisa without thinking. Then she adds, "We have a variety of art classes."

He looks straight at her and says, "I'd like to apply for a gallery show."

She blinks. "Well, we don't have an application for that. It's by invitation only," she says in what she hopes is a kind tone. She wonders whether he may have rehearsed this request. It's surprising that the son of Heinrich and Agatha Steiger doesn't know the most basic of art world protocols.

"How can I get invited?"

He stands before her like a soldier, knees locked and shoulders back. It's this kind of confidence that bewilders Louisa, the kind of male determination based on nothing but the itch of potential inside. The kind of sureness that if indulged, turns into arrogance. If neglected, it can become despair, even nihilism. There have been countless generations of boys like this, and there will always be more. They replicate themselves, always reaching for the same thing.

She pauses before answering, which probably gives him hope. "First you need a body of work."

"I have one."

"And a national or regional reputation."

He sucks his lower lip. "But how can I get a reputation without a show?"

She smiles. "That's a good question."

"What about the residency?"

"Well, we're not really ready for that yet. There's a new studio on the property, but applications probably won't open until next year."

"Who's there now?"

"No one. The building's not finished yet."

He drops one shoulder, stands at a tilt, and looks up at the vaulted ceiling, at Richard's beams and skylights.

"I need more space to work," he says, looking back at Louisa. "I want to do large-scale projects."

"An art class might be just the thing," she says. "Would you like a tour of the center?"

"No." He looks up to the ceiling again. "No, that's not necessary."

"Well, you can sign up for a class, or if you decide you want a tour you can come back anytime we're open." She walks toward the door, conscious of his eyes on her.

"Louisa."

Something catches in her stomach. She turns. He stares at her, lips set together. If she were a young girl, she'd already be hopelessly lost.

5.

O NCE LOUISA IS on the train, once the doors have
closed and the platform has receded, momentum
overtakes her. She keeps her mind empty as she
looks out the window at the ratcheting trees, the creeks
jungled with trash. Through the press of flesh in Grand
Central, she descends the escalator, takes the subway downtown, and comes back up to an alien city. Her thighs stick
together as she walks, chafing beneath her black pencil skirt.
The skirt is foolishly confining. She regrets whatever nar-
cissism made her choose it and the slingback Ferragamo
sandals. She hasn't really stopped long enough to consider
the wisdom of this trip, at all. If she had, she wouldn't have
left home. She would have allowed the weights of habit, of
stagnation, to anchor her. But there's no art in that. There's
no sense of life in that.

Buildings exhale heat from their bricks. A crowd is gathered outside Bernard Stirling, and Louisa weaves her way
inside. There are so many young people drinking wine from

plastic cups, working their stops on the gallery circuit. They make little pretense of viewing the art but stand in muttering bunches, glancing at their phones. To Louisa they seem more jaded than ever, already past the crest of youth when ideas are playful and raw. They're in such a rush to mature, to exhaust everything. It's art school, maybe, that does it. Or technology, the nonstop pressure to be seen and shared, to post and be posted.

It takes no more than five minutes to look at the art, which is, after all, balls on the floor. The white walls are blank. The artist stands in the gallery's center, her sharp bootheels among the red orbs. It's clearly acceptable to disrupt their placement; perhaps kicking is even encouraged, part of the viewing experience. Louisa picks one up and examines it. It's made of polyurethane, a seam running around the circumference. A cheap rubber ball.

Louisa isn't yet ready to approach Angelica. She lingers near the artist catalogue at the reception desk and feels her eyes pulled toward the door. She understands, even as she hasn't admitted it to herself, that she's waiting for Xavier. At one point, she almost believes she sees him, a tall skinny figure with his back to her, hands in sagging jean pockets. Her pulse quickens even as her brain knows its mistake. The boy who turns and walks past can't be more than twenty.

At last, Louisa steps away from the wall and lets Angelica notice her. Their eyes meet and Angelica smiles faintly before looking back to the man with whom she's speaking. She's the same but sunken in the face now—the red lips and spiked hair even more severe against her caved features. She looks, at last, like a serious artist.

Louisa finds Bernard, who kisses her cheek. "What do you think?" he asks.

Bernard is handsome and honest, good to his artists. He must be truly upset about Xavier's troubles. He's seen so many go the same way. Louisa knows it's something he never gets used to.

"It's about what I expected." Louisa smiles.

At that moment, Angelica appears and puts a hand to her shoulder. "I haven't seen you in for*ever*," she says with the same hoarseness in her voice that for all Louisa knows is no longer put-on.

"I don't come down very often. And when I do, I usually avoid all this."

"But not this time." Angelica smiles. "How's Connecticut?" She distinctly pronounces each syllable.

"Green, quiet."

Louisa pauses. She considers giving Angelica a compliment on her work, a meager lie, but the inclination to congratulate her is gone. It's possible, even likely, that Angelica is still in touch with Xavier. They were always close. Louisa has always had her suspicions.

"It's good to see you're still working." That's as much as she offers.

"Still working, yes," Angelica repeats offhandedly, cocking her head as she scrutinizes Louisa's face. There's no hint of animosity in her now. Whatever rivalry had existed between them went slack long ago. Angelica has won.

"I admire that," Louisa says.

Angelica smiles. "Thank you, Louisa. Not everyone keeps going, as you know. Not everyone is as blockheaded as I am."

"You've always been driven."

Angelica puts a hand to Louisa's shoulder. "Xavier's here tonight. He'll want to see you."

Louisa doesn't respond. It's as if the touch of Angelica's hand has turned her to stone.

"I'll see if I can flag him down."

Louisa is overtaken by the urge to run out of the gallery. She could pivot now, without a word, and just go. It would be bad to see Xavier, disastrous. Although the secret hope of seeing him is, in fact, what's brought her here, she knows it can't lead to anything but pain. Why would she want to see him, fallen? Why would she want to show herself, fallen further?

It's too late. Against all odds, the two of them are in this room together, and he's coming toward her. The sight of him returns like lost music: the angled shoulders, the long narrow waist. His eyes meet hers, and his face lights up. This smile of his is a rarity, a grand event. He reaches her in three strides and wraps her in his arms with startling force.

"Louisa, Louisa, Louisa," he says into her hair.

He releases her and draws back. His smile is already fading. He stands in front of her in his entirety and they face each other like mutually conjured ghosts.

"It's so great to see you here," Louisa says, "supporting Angelica."

"Angelica, yeah."

They continue to stand. Xavier's eyes are still the best part of his face, of the room, of the city. Their first morning together, they'd awoken on the mattress in her apartment beneath the stucco ceiling. Music had been playing from above, some delicate forlorn tune, Neil Young or Nick Drake. It had taken a moment for Louisa to register the body holding down the other side of the mattress, to remember she wasn't alone. It had taken another moment to recall the club on Gansevoort Street, to connect it with the shape of this man facing away from her in the winter morning light. His vertebrae were prominent, like the dorsal bones of some primeval sea creature. He'd turned slowly and faced her, his eyes a bright attack. Those eyes, she sensed, would never stop being new.

He's even taller than she remembers and far too thin. The protruding jaw and sloped forehead are extreme, almost ugly. When she last saw him, he was selling paintings for $100,000. He'd been in the Whitney Biennial. Now, the insides of his arms are punctured and striped like battle maps. He's done nothing to hide it. The sight makes her lightheaded, and she forces herself to keep her eyes on his face.

"Have you been working?" she asks.

"Not really. I live with some kids in Red Hook who let me stay for free. They're great. But things haven't been going so well." He blinks slowly. "I'm actually thinking of leaving the city."

"To go where?"

He looks down at the red balls. "I don't know. Maybe the suburbs like you."

"What would you do in the suburbs?"

"I don't know. Live in a house. Mow the lawn. Have a dog." He laughs, pulls his eyes back up to her. "What do *you* do in the suburbs?"

She takes a breath. "I run the art center in town. I'm married. I have a daughter."

"I'll probably never have children."

This seems an obvious fact. The more she looks at him, the less healthy he appears. It occurs to her that he may in fact be truly, drastically sick. How can this be? She remembers him naked, pressed down on her, their hearts hammering in synch. Maybe he's remembering, too, how they'd once folded and fused. Nothing was to be trusted, she'd once thought, if not the permanence of their eye lock, the flutter of lash on her face.

"Who did you marry?" he asks.

"An architect."

"What's he like?"

"He's a good person, very stable. Very smart and successful."

There's a long pause.

"So, you're not working, then," Louisa says. "I mean, on your own work."

He doesn't reply. Perhaps his past success seems trivial now, not worth remembering. She wonders if his roommates know who he is and if that's why they're letting him stay. Or maybe they think they're just being kind to an anonymous aging hipster, a dinosaur. Maybe he's a joke to them, a warning of what not to become.

Xavier stares at Louisa, pulling the space tight between them. The moment stretches until it flips inside out, and she forgets where she is and when. She imagines the two of them falling to the floor in one motion. In her mind, she slides a hand under his shirt and presses her fingers to his chest.

"Louisa," he says in a rough voice, and time springs back into place.

"I'm sorry," she mutters, "I have to go say hello to someone. I'll be back."

She isn't sure how she pulls away from his stare, how she makes it to the door. When she turns to look back, he's in the same place, watching her. Outside on the sidewalk, the heat of the concrete coming through her shoe soles, she feels dazed. She doesn't remember making the decision to come, can't recall how she arrived in the city. It's as if she's been sleepwalking and has just now awoken.

Humidity rests like hot breath on her skin, the gravid air that precedes a storm.

In the train car back north, the temperature is far below that of her body, which has absorbed all the heat of the day—the midsummer city heat that's almost palpable, full of invisible circuits that connect strangers. She replays the encounter with Xavier. She rearranges it in every way she can imagine. She clutches him, she assaults him, she takes his hand and leads him out of the gallery. She avoids him altogether. She misses the train, stays in Nearwater.

Finally, as the city recedes behind her, she finds her mind drifting from Xavier to the Steiger boy. She wonders if he's already made himself at home in the residency cabin, if he's been there all day in the heat. There's no air-conditioning installed yet, not even a fan. She remembers the ambivalence she'd felt, leading him there. It had been hard to think straight as he waited for her offer, his black hair and shirt absorbing the sun. She'd told him it wasn't an official residency, that he wasn't to advertise it. But no one ever came out there, and he'd have privacy. She wouldn't even mention it to the staff. It had felt illicit, showing him the cabin, giving him the key.

Back home, Richard is still awake, the light still on in his office. All at once, the house feels sterile to her, Richard hermetic, and Nearwater unbearably quiet. Countless days of her life have been lost in this fairy-tale quicksand, this soft illusion of bliss. Comfort is the only goal in this town—the kind of bland, coddling comfort meant for children. Grown people need friction to live.

Richard hears Louisa come home. He's been having trouble focusing on his reading, going over the same line again and again: "If man were a beast or an angel, he would not be able to be in anxiety. Since he is both beast and angel, he can be in anxiety, and the greater the anxiety, the greater the man." The words alight in his consciousness but refuse to sink in. His mind keeps returning to Sylvie and the awkward dinner they'd had together.

He puts down the book when Louisa appears in the doorway of his office.

"How was the city?" he asks.

"The show was a disappointment. Nothing's changed, really."

Richard looks at her standing there, leaning against the jamb in her sleek clothing. Sometimes, when he returns from a business trip, when they've been separated for some time, she appears briefly unfamiliar to him. She reverts to the stranger she'd been when they first met, a beguiling dark-haired sphinx—a locked capsule he'd wanted to both preserve and crack open.

"Angelica's still the same bitch," she says.

Richard nods, though he's not that interested. Talking to his wife can be like talking to a teenager at times. In marrying her, he may have cracked open the capsule but not all its contents are surprising.

"How was your night?" she asks.

"Not great," he says. "I'm worried about Sylvie. I tried to talk to her at dinner and barely got one-word responses."

"Well, she's never been a great conversationalist. She's just a quiet kid."

Richard grimaces. "I think something's changed. We used to be able to talk more easily. She always used to tell me all about her day or at least about the horses at the barn. Now, nothing. I'm afraid she's depressed or anxious."

"Please don't catastrophize. She's a preteen. All kids pull away when they hit puberty. You know that. If anything, it's just going to get worse, so buckle up."

Richard looks grimly at her. "How do we know it's normal? What if it's not?"

He does his best to describe their dinner, how he'd tried to tease her out, make her laugh, but she'd just shrugged. She'd barely eaten half her pasta. Richard has heard about children being troubled these days as no children have ever been in history. The numbers are staggering: the mental health struggles, the depression and suicide. They're akin to adult numbers, or worse. This disaster isn't tied to war or poverty but more covert, insidious things. Technology addiction, the glut of information and image, the constant suck of consumerism. The thousand cuts of social pressure. He's afraid that some hidden rot has begun inside their daughter.

"I don't know what's going on, but I'm worried she's see-ing things on the internet."

"Like what?"

Richard is quiet. His suspicion is that Sylvie's trouble is linked to some online rumor, some social contagion they have no way of detecting. He's heard of a few of these but only after they'd surfaced in the mainstream media, after they were already obsolete. He knows about the meme of a terrifying bird-woman chimera, a sculpture created by a Japanese artist and co-opted by bad actors. He read that the bird-woman had been appearing in videos aimed at children and giving directives—whether outright or subliminal he's not sure—to kill themselves. It seems some children had done so. Louisa assured him this was an urban legend, but he isn't convinced.

"I don't know," he answers. "She wouldn't talk about it."

"When does she ever talk?"

Richard knows Louisa means this earnestly, but it sounds harsh. As his wife stands in the doorway, he has the impres-sion that she's not fully there. She's still buzzing from the city. He senses, as he often does, that she's experienced some-thing independent of him that she can't or won't share.

"We shouldn't have gotten her that phone," Richard says. "I was against it."

"I know."

He was stung by how Louisa had overridden his concern. Like all younger people, she minimizes the perspective that comes with age. The old values maintain a tighter grip on his generation than on hers. And it really is a generation— nearly twenty years—that divides them.

"We should at least be checking her search history. And we should install one of those tracking features they have now that lets you see where the phone is at any time."

"Richard, we've talked about this. We don't want to spy."

"I think you're being naïve. Kids need guardrails with this kind of technology. They're too young to know what to do with so much stimulus. It's a cesspool of smut and lies. Even adults fall prey to unsavory things."

They've been over it a hundred times. Richard knows she's exasperated with him, that she thinks he's out of touch. He's a proud Luddite, even using pencil and paper for his initial architectural drawings, to his employees' chagrin.

"It's part of the culture now," Louisa says from the doorway. "It's not going away, so you're going to have to get used to it, and Sylvie's going to need to adapt. Our job is to give her the tools, not take them from her."

Richard knows he'll defer to his wife again, as he does in so many aspects of parenthood. By virtue of her youth and sex—and his frequent absences—she's more closely aligned with their daughter, the one with boots on the ground. He feels somewhat helpless in this regard. But he'd insisted on the biggest decisions: settling in Nearwater, choosing this plot of land. He'd wanted a safe place for a family, insulated from the coarse influence of popular culture. He felt he'd earned the privilege of choosing the soundest, most exclusive environment to raise his child. And Nearwater is beyond anything he could have dreamed of as a boy. Its history is stunning to him, grown from seed as he was in the pioneer Midwest. There are antique houses out of picture books with properties so perfect—willows, waterfalls, ponds—they're like pieces of Eden. But when Sylvie gazes into her phone, he expects she's not in Nearwater.

"I'm going to bed," Louisa says, moving out of the doorway.

Richard feels slightly abashed. He knows he overreacts, that he lets his imagination get the better of him. Maybe she's right when she tells him to relax, that every generation worries about the one that follows. Every cultural shift seems to portend the end of the species. He'll accept it eventually, just as his own grandparents had accepted television, the streaming of strangers into their living rooms. He'll adapt, or he won't. It really doesn't matter in the end.

6.

T HE CABIN IS filled with creatures. The boy wears
safety glasses while cutting them out of plywood
with an electric saw. He carries the buckets of paint
by hand from his basement studio all the way through the
woods. He works all night and comes back to his parents'
house at dawn, speckled with color. In the quiet kitchen, he
pours a bowl of cereal and sits at the granite counter. While
he eats, he posts his process photos: just scraps of image,
mysterious and compelling, the painted eyes of animals,
uncaptioned. Comments appear:

So spooky and beautiful! More, please.

He sees a comment from the girl: *Awesome.*

Then, a direct message: *What are you making?*

He writes back: *It's going to be a public installation. A boat surrounded by animals cut out of wood. I'm going to splash them with black
paint to look like oil.*

She responds: *Wow, that's so cool. Do you need help?*

He pauses, then types: *Sure.*

I can come tonight.

He stares at the phone.

Is it okay if I come?

Yes, of course. But can you get dropped off? I don't want anyone else to see it before it's done.

Don't worry I'll come by myself. I'll ride my bike.

He hesitates. Then he tells her where to find him.

The girl seems an invention of the night itself, pale in the light that shines over the cabin door.

"How did you get out?" the boy asks her.

She smiles, coming inside. "I'm quiet."

"I'm impressed."

"Oh, wow," she says when she sees the animals, already sawn and shaped from plywood. There are two of each, at least four feet across: sloths, armadillos, jaguars.

"They're the animals from the Amazon wildfires," he tells her. "I'm making an ark for them. Sort of a life-size version of the miniature one I showed you in my studio."

"I heard about the fires." She looks at him where he stands in the middle of the room with a paintbrush. He wears paint-smeared jeans and a black T-shirt with a curious symbol, like a distorted capital *H*.

"What does your shirt mean?" she asks.

He looks down at the symbol. "Oh. That's the Norse rune of disruption. It's the logo for an activist group." He tells her what they do, environmental actions and interventions. "Sometimes people get arrested," he says.

"Have you been arrested?"

He laughs. "Not yet." He hands her a paintbrush. "Here. First we paint them realistically. I'll show you how."

He begins with a piglike animal that he calls a tapir. She chooses a jaguar. She loads the brush with gold paint, and a few drops hit the floor.

"Go ahead, just slap it on," he tells her.

She makes the first stroke, a diagonal stripe across the animal's flank. She looks at him and smiles.

"Beautiful," he says and smiles back.

The cabin is dimly lit by a floor lamp plugged into a rudimentary outlet. The wiring is visible, veins and arteries running between exposed studs.

"I read about the Amazon fires online," the girl says. "I saw the pictures."

The boy stares at the tapir, the feathered strokes he's been making to imitate fur. He looks at the girl beside him, painting. "The animals are being burned alive," he tells her. "Even the monkeys aren't fast enough. Nobody understands how bad it is. Or they don't want to know. It's so much easier to live in denial. The Amazon's already contaminated from drilling to begin with. The plants and animals are full of poison from all the waste the oil companies have been dumping. Even the rainforest tribes have cadmium and lead in their blood. And nobody even knows or cares."

"What?"

"See? People don't know."

"But if you know, other people must know."

He huffs. "Yeah, except the people who try to do something about it tend to get killed."

He keeps talking. His voice resonates in the cabin. It's human nature to block things out, he tells her. When events are too big to absorb, people pretend they're not happening. It's much easier, more natural, to focus on the small, immediate things we can control. It's easier to carry a reusable grocery bag and recycle wine bottles.

"Are your parents like that?" he asks.

"Yeah," she says.

"Mine too. They're all like that. That's why we have to shock them out of their dream lives."

He talks about the corporations that pretend to play along, making "green" products packaged in plastic, using fossil fuels to produce them. He condemns the bourgeoisie with their hybrid cars and their kids who make posters for school about saving the Earth and then buy plastic crap from China. Meanwhile, humans keep multiplying, razing the forests, building and building. The ocean is dying, forests are dying, animals are dying forever. He talks about the Pacific garbage gyre and the disappearance of bees. Greenhouse gases, offshore drilling, tanker spills.

He stops painting for a minute. "Did you know the Amazon fires are being intentionally set? They're clearing land for cows to graze so that they can be turned into meat."

The girl stops painting too. "They're setting the fires on purpose? Who is?"

"The farmers. The meat companies."

She stares. "I believe you, but I can't believe it's true. If it were true, someone would do something. Wouldn't somebody punish them?"

"Who?"

"I don't know. The police. Or God."

"But no one's doing anything. No one's paying attention," he says, his voice rising. "No god or human. No one except you and me."

"You and me?"

He looks somberly at her. "Maybe we're the humans. Maybe we're the gods."

She listens. She paints slowly, meticulously, and they work for a while without talking. Then, without warning, she says, "Do you have sisters or brothers?"

"No," the boy answers.

"Me neither. Sometimes I wish I did."

"Why?"

She shrugs. "Someone to talk to. That's all, I guess."

He stops painting for a second and looks at her. Her face is serious, half-lit by the floor lamp beside them. One side bright, the other in shadow.

"You can talk to me."

She doesn't answer.

"Is there something you want to talk about?"

She stares at the wooden jaguar in front of her. "I have a friend who died."

She tells him that the friend was the same age she is now. She tells him how and why she died. She tells him that they finally dug up the toxic junk from under the sports field, but that the adults on the school board are still in charge. They're still making decisions.

"That's what I'm talking about," the boy snarls. "That's exactly what I mean. Their own kids are dying, but they close their eyes like it isn't happening."

"I keep thinking about how she looked when I saw her the last time, in her nightgown with this ruffled collar." She takes a deep breath. "Nobody even got punished."

She doesn't look at him, but her face tightens. Her eyes squint a little, and she tilts her head as if she's studying the jaguar. The corners of her mouth tug down. Her face crumples, and she covers it with her hands. For a moment, she stands still, then her body is overtaken by sobs. She lowers herself to the floor, huddles inward.

"I'm sorry," she says between gasps. "I don't know what's wrong with me."

"It's okay," the boy says, standing in place. He leans down and puts a hand to her shoulder. "It's okay."

It takes a few minutes for her to collect herself. Once she does, she stands up straighter, with a new kind of poise.

She tells him that back when her friend was sick, she'd found lumps beneath her own nipples. Hard flat discs, like buttons. She could grab onto them. Every day she hoped the lumps might have disappeared, but they just got bigger and harder. She was convinced it was cancer. Instead of worrying her parents, she kept it to herself for months. For those months, she'd been obsessed with death.

"I kept thinking about how when I died, life would go on without me, all the everyday things. The sun, caterpillars, hot laundry. I wondered what it would feel like to die. Would it be like being crushed or like fading away?"

And then her friend had done it. It was like she'd leaped from the diving board and disappeared, leaving her waiting on the ladder.

Finally, the girl went to her mother in a bashful babyish way and said something vague about her worry. Her mother took her to the doctor to discuss it, and that was that. Later, she understood that the growing lumps were normal, of course, but she'd inadvertently touched a cold truth.

After a long silence, the boy says, "Well, just remember that death is natural. All animals die and sink back into the earth and get absorbed by other things. Plants grow out of our bodies, and we become part of the organisms that eat us. So, we're immortal, really."

The girl stands with her arms at her sides, paintbrush hanging down, dripping gold paint onto the floor. She stares straight ahead at the jaguar. "My friend said she wasn't afraid."

"That's good," he says. "If you aren't afraid, then you can be at peace about it. You can be happy to go back into nature and become whatever's next."

The girl nods. "They planted a tree for her at the cemetery. Maybe it's growing out of her body now. I don't know. But I still think it was stupid, planting a tree. Like that was supposed to make us feel better. Instead of actually apologizing. Instead of admitting that it was their fault."

"You want them to apologize."

She doesn't look at him. "I want them to fix it."

"No one fixes anything unless we make them fix it."

She looks at him.

"You should go home," he says. "It's really late. But listen." He comes up next to her. "Listen. It's good to remember that you're dying. We have to remember all the time, every minute. We could be killed any second. The world could be destroyed. No, actually we *are* being killed every second, and the world *is* being destroyed. We need to remember and keep going." He points to the deer skull nestled in the corner of the room. "That's why I keep that thing. To help remember that I'm an animal. They say animals aren't aware of their mortality the way humans are, but really it's the other way around. So just remember you're an animal and you're dying. Now, and now, and now."

As the girl goes outside, the sky is just beginning to brighten. She rides home with her headlamp, pedaling into its narrow peninsula of light. She doesn't stop pedaling, doesn't stop to consider the nocturnal activity in the margins of her sight, the toothed and clawed threats. If there's a predator in the woods—animal or human—it will have to chase her. She moves forward until she arrives at the mouth of her driveway. She slips soundlessly into the house, climbs the stairs like a spirit. In bed, she lies awake for a long time. She doesn't sleep but instead stares at the walls of her bedroom, so much like a satin-lined box. She lies there until her window shade is edged with morning sun.

7.

L OUISA WAKES TO a flare, a fan opening inside her. It's like what she sometimes felt in New York when first opening her eyes to her dirty apartment, the stucco ceiling and limp ivy plant hanging overhead. Now she sees a smooth ceiling, clean white paint. Fine dust motes hover in a band of sunlight. Her husband is already awake beside her. Saturday. She drowsily tries to locate the source of the flush—something new and colorful—and the memory of seeing Xavier comes back in a seasick rush.

The day looms in front of her. She drags herself into the office, where she attempts to update the center's social media accounts. Deirdre arrives in red leather pants, and Louisa nods hello. She's resisted handing the social media job to Deirdre, although it would be so much easier. Deirdre would know what levers to push. Louisa watches her settle in at her desk and recognizes a twitch of envy in herself, a competitive kind of scrutiny. The girl is attractive, but in a way that leads straight to sex, the kind of allure that fades quickly.

"Whose camera is that?" Deirdre asks, glancing at the Leica on Louisa's desk.

"Mine."

The girl looks bemused but doesn't press further, for which Louisa is grateful. Louisa doesn't want to talk about photography now. There's a kind of negative juice traveling her veins. Sometimes, sitting at her desk, she feels disoriented, as if she's abruptly awoken from a deep sleep and surfaced in the wrong life. When had she agreed to come sit at this desk every day? How did it happen that she has a daughter in a swimming pool a mile away—and a mile in the other direction, a husband? When had these people appeared? When had her life become glued to theirs?

Usually, when Louisa returns to her glass canister house after work, she's soothed by it, but today she's perturbed. There aren't enough places to sit. There are no invitations to activity, no comforting temptations. There are only so many baths a woman can take, only so many magazines, only so much phone scrolling. The evenings pass one into another. After each week is done, Louisa feels that it was effortless—that the time has somehow passed effortlessly.

After work, she stands in the kitchen and makes a Cobb salad for dinner. Sylvie is still in her wet bathing suit, wearing a towel and eating cereal from the box. Louisa is at a loss when it comes to certain aspects of raising a child. If she nags, she hates herself. If she says nothing, she hates herself. She watches her daughter fist the cereal into her mouth, in need of its cheap energy. Maybe she'll still become a vigorous girl. She seems to be in a good mood today, thankfully, temporarily a child again.

"I talked to Hannah Warren," Sylvie says between bites. "She said Katherine's parents are starting a scholarship fund in her name for kids at the hunt club."

"What a nice idea," says Louisa, before horror has a chance to invade her voice. What family would ever want their child to win such a scholarship? She smiles at Sylvie. Her daughter is young and hungry, and Louisa feels a stroke of gratification. They've given her a house that's spacious and cool, in a safe part of the country. What fortune they enjoy. What a success she's made of her life, after all.

When her phone rings with an unknown number, she answers without thinking, expecting a robocall. Instead, a man's voice says, "Louisa?"

"Hello?"

"It's Bernard."

His voice is dry, as if he's been speaking all day. She holds back and lets him continue.

"I'm calling with bad news."

There's a suspended moment. "Xavier?"

"I'm sorry," says Bernard. "This is a very hard phone call to make."

Louisa holds the phone to her ear and stares at the stovetop, at the black Viking burners that look like spiders. He'd been missing for a number of days, Bernard tells her, before the roommates bothered to investigate. No one knows how long he'd been gone. They found him, finally, on the roof of the building.

Nausea rises in Louisa, and she braces herself against it. She imagines gathering it inward, away from the walls of her stomach. She takes a breath and holds it. "This is terrible," she says. "But not a complete shock."

She doesn't ask for more. She thanks Bernard for calling, tells him to get some rest. There's no one else to make the calls, he explains, no immediate relatives. There'll be a notice in the paper and the magazines, he says. Louisa thanks him again and hangs up.

The kitchen hums around her. The salad spinner waits on the counter where she left it, wet lettuce poking through the holes of the plastic cage. At that moment, it's a foreign object, its use unknown. Louisa concentrates on breathing, keeping the ball of nausea intact as she holds the salad spinner over the sink and pushes its wide rubber button. It makes a whirring sound. She takes off the lid and pours the yellow water, the shreds of vegetable matter, into the drain.

That evening, she and Richard sit in the screened porch. Louisa rests on the wire-grid Bertoia chair, a snifter of cognac at her side. Richard sits in a floating black disc chair that's supported by one curved leg, like a spoon bent backward. He reclines with his arms crossed. The fireflies pulse sluggishly, out of synch, as if too tired to live the few weeks remaining to them. Soon the trees will grow dry and shed themselves clean, and the house will be naked in snow. But for now, the summer weeks blend together. Louisa, Richard, and Sylvie perform the motions of their days slowly in the heat, like swimmers making leisurely laps. Summer expands and holds open so wide that it seems it might never close again.

As they sit in the porch, Louisa breathes through the sickness that's still in her stomach while Richard tells her about a new commission for Caspar Von Mauren, the Liechtensteiner, who wants a birdlike guesthouse. This is no surprise to Louisa. Europeans love Richard. Most Americans prefer their guesthouses to match their colonials; they don't want the shape of a bird. Next week, he'll be going to Paris to consult with another client for a few days. As he talks, Louisa feels the span of the ocean already opening between them. She looks at him in the faint light. He's the type of man who ages well, with a strong brow and hair like Cary Grant's, grayed only at the temples. Louisa sometimes forgets how dramatically handsome he is. There are women who'd want him. Minty women in Vineyard Vines are no threat here in Nearwater, but outside the town limits are real women with greedy minds and bodies. Louisa believes he's too inward a man to fall prey to this. He's a man who makes decisions and moves on, who fastens on one thing at a time. She'd been Richard's decision.

The demise of his first marriage had made him value her even more. He never could have sat quietly like this with his first wife, whose need for reassurance had soured everything. Richard loves how little validation Louisa needs. They've rarely discussed their exes, and she'd only told him about Xavier in vague terms. She'd abandoned him in his downward spiral is how she explained it, having simply grown up faster than he had.

"How are things at the center?" Richard asks her now.

"The same," Louisa hears herself answer in a light voice. She's sometimes amazed at how easily she can pull this voice up. "Summer's always half-dead. But we're almost ready for the gala, at least. I was thinking of inviting the Steigers, to see if we might get them involved. What do you think? I know it's not up to their level, but it seems like a shame not to try. I mean, it's their local art venue. We should at least extend the invitation."

"Absolutely."

"I'll send them tickets. Maybe I'll seat them with the Von Maurens."

"So they can all complain about my work?"

"So they can talk about European things, castles and knights. Anyway, I'm excited about next year. I have some ideas for artists to bring in."

"Anyone I've heard of?"

"Well, no, I don't know. I don't want to jinx it."

"Surprise me, then. I'm sure it'll be great."

Richard's faith in Louisa is a mystery to her, based on nothing she's earned. She decides not to tell him that it's her own work she hopes to exhibit: her secret new series, fragmentary images of society people. Whether these belong at the art center or somewhere better she hasn't yet decided, but somehow sharing any of it with Richard is embarrassing. Perhaps it's not faith he has in her but rather disinterest. He'd been vocally impressed by her photographs when they first met. They were part of her downtown appeal for him, along with her looks and youth and artist friends. But in the years since he hasn't asked to see more. The fact that she stopped taking pictures, that she voluntarily sank into motherhood and work, must seem proof that she's moved past it. He has no reason to think art has ever been anything more than a hobby for her.

The first time she boarded the train to New York with her camera, she was a senior in college, twenty-one years old. She'd been to the city many times before, of course, with her parents and friends, but had never made the trip solo. Her friend Noelle was living on MacDougal Street after graduating, and Louisa had promised to visit. The train ride from college was two hours. She looked through the scratched window at the grimy backs of houses that faced the train tracks. Poughkeepsie had seen better days. Once the train cleared city limits, the view turned green, and budding trees sped past.

She remembers how the train had seemed particularly bleak in contrast with the spring day, the yellow interior light making the passengers look sickly. An old man in the row across the aisle seemed to be asleep, his body bunched in the corner of the seat, his hatted head against the window. Louisa had drawn out her camera and quietly focused it, framing him in the lower corner and letting the windowpane blur. The shutter had bitten down excruciatingly slowly, loudly, but the man hadn't stirred. She'd watched him, looking for signs of respiration, suddenly afraid he was dead. There was something thrilling about the possibility that she may have just photographed a dead man. The idea bubbled up as a dark anecdote for the future—a twist she'd include in interviews, signaling her auspicious beginnings as an artist—but then the man's hand moved, a little flutter against his pant leg, and he'd shifted and scratched his ear.

Louisa had turned away and aimed the camera at her own bare legs. She thought of Robert Mapplethorpe as she zoomed in on her thighs and watched them melt into abstractions. She held her breath and waited for the picture to latch into place and become compulsory. Something happened at that ephemeral instant when, through the viewfinder, the distance between eye and subject vanished.

It felt almost sexual, like building to orgasm, the precise moment to take the picture. None of the theoretical texts from her art history classes described this phenomenon. She'd thought about writing an honors thesis on it but had changed her mind. It was more important to take the pictures than to talk about taking them.

That weekend was going to be her breakthrough. She was going to finish her entire senior project in one streak. She was going to step into Nan Goldin's shoes, document the guts of the city, the part that suburbanites never saw, the musty dives and the creatures that came out at night like glittered serpents—the fabled underworld that Noelle said she'd seen.

And she'd done it. That weekend, and nearly every weekend after, she'd come down on the train with her camera until she graduated—with a degree in art history, to her parents' dismay—and moved downtown herself. With her teenage modeling portfolio in hand, it proved easy enough to find jobs. She was busier than she'd expected to be and more successful. Finding little in common with the other models—or not wanting to—she went to gallery openings and underground clubs. She discovered the art scene but never felt completely part of it. She sensed that to the artists she was a hanger-on, a dilletante, a pretty accoutrement. Her beauty was itself suspect.

The fireflies pulse low to the ground in silent communication and give Louisa a tug of regret. It hits her again that Xavier is gone, and the thing that had existed between them—blooming and spreading and rotting—is gone now too. Richard is deep in his own thoughts, focused on something far past the porch screen, past the lawn and the trees beyond. He doesn't know what's in her mind, and she doesn't know what's in his. She knows, though, that they're both affected by this sliver of time before nightfall. This is something they share, and she's glad not to have to explain. One of the things she loves about him is his capacity for quiet, his disinclination to intrude, his respect for moments like these.

"I heard something really disturbing yesterday," Richard says in the dark. "When I was doing the walk-through with James Gray, we were talking about our kids, and he told me that they had to take their daughter's phone away. They found out that strange men were messaging her and asking her for nude pictures."

"What? That's crazy. How old is she?"

"Twelve."

"My God."

Richard takes a sip of cognac, clears his throat. "The thing is, she was sending them the pictures."

Louisa looks at him.

"We have to be more careful, Louisa. We can't just assume none of this will happen to us. If it can happen to Maeve Gray, it can happen to any kid. Are there controls we can put on Sylvie's phone? Does she use these apps?"

Louisa sighs, shakes her head. A tension headache has begun at the base of her neck.

"Also, a phone tracker."

"I don't think that's a good idea, Richard."

"Why not?" His voice rises. "Wouldn't you feel better, knowing where she is? Wouldn't you feel safer, limiting who she can contact? These are basic precautions. I'm sure the Grays wish they'd done it."

"I understand, but I just think it would end up being counterproductive. We can't give her freedom with one hand and then police her with the other."

"But she's a child."

"I'm telling you, she'll resent us if we don't respect her privacy."

"So, you don't check her phone at all?"

"I do check it sometimes," Louisa lies.

Richard looks pointedly at her for a moment. "Good. It's our responsibility to do that. We have to be vigilant."

"Don't worry," she says. "Sylvie's a good kid. She knows not to talk to strangers in real life, and the same goes for online. She has common sense. But if I ever saw anything unusual, of course I'd intervene."

What Louisa doesn't say is that she's terrified of Sylvie looking at her the way she'd looked at her own mother when she'd discovered that her mother had been reading her diary. Any trust between them had been shattered forever. Their job as parents isn't to monitor but to prepare. They have to let her learn to navigate the world. They have to be single-minded in this, girded against fear.

Louisa, too, had been an only child, an obedient daughter. Her inner life was a fire she'd kept secretly kindled until the day she left Nearwater, until she finally joined the anonymous ranks of the city, the legions of the beautiful and afflicted. It was the extraordinary she was after, the sublime. She wanted to capture it in her art and claim a slice of immortality. This chance was only available to those who deliberately sought it. It didn't manifest for people like her parents, whose days were spent in offices, brokering trivial deals, complacent and asleep. Sublimity died in the presence of paranoia and control. No matter what happens now, she won't fall into that mire. She'll be a different kind of adult, a gentler, respectful parent, her face turned to the light.

They sit for a while, as they do every evening until the brandy is drained. Then, when Louisa goes up to bed, Richard retreats to his office to read his leatherbound sets of Nietzsche and Hegel and Kierkegaard. He sits in a spartan wooden chair—anything more comfortable would lull him to sleep, he says—and unravels one sentence at a time about eternal recurrence, *Weltgeist*, the paradox of faith. These are the kinds of dense, forbidding books she tried—and failed—to read in college.

Tonight, she stirs when Richard comes into bed. She opens her eyes to watch him lie down carefully beside her. She asks him about his reading, as she does from time to time, if only to demonstrate her interest in him. He makes a stumbling effort to explain Kierkegaard's *Either/Or*, the aesthetic and ethical stages of life. It's difficult for her to follow these threads, especially late at night, which is why she seldom asks.

"Sounds like you're in the ethical stage, but I'm still in the aesthetic one," she offers, smiling.

"There's another stage too. Kierkegaard calls it the knight of faith, someone who's able to grasp the finite and the infinite at the same time. Complete hopelessness and complete faith. It's supposed to be a paradox, an impossible leap. To do it would take perfect naïveté or idiocy, a preposterous cleanness of mind. In other words, insanity."

"Or maybe just youth," Louisa adds.

Richard stares for a moment. "But if you think about it," he says, "it's what we all have to do to get through every day without losing our minds. How do we hold despair in one hand and the will to persist in the other?"

A disconcerting vibration comes into his voice, and his eyes take on a remote, tunneling quality. He is, in so many ways, as clean and light as his architecture. Simple, considered: rich wood and large windows, wide, angular light. But at times like these Louisa also glimpses a sequestered depth, an umbrous pond. She understands there are hidden strata in each of them that the other has never visited. To plumb every fissure would be exploitative, unsustainable to marriage.

Early in their courtship they'd gone to Central Park, and Louisa had brought her camera. The first time she aimed the lens at him, he was flustered. He tried to relax after that, to be playful for her benefit. He posed on a bench and crossed his eyes for the camera. She'd shrieked and clicked the shutter. All those green park benches were there, in the backgrounds of the negatives she'd developed, now snugly tucked away in the closet. When she first looked at the photographs, she'd been struck by the rows of figures on those benches, people talking, reading books, looking away. They'd all been together in the park that day—she, Richard, and these people on green benches. While Louisa and her future husband had been playing out their script, what dramas had been unfolding around them? What's happened to those people since? Their clothing would now be outdated. How many are still in New York, still coming to sit in the park? How many are dead? How many have known great joy since that day, or pain? The elderly woman with the pigeon at her feet, the rolled socks—Louisa makes herself stop thinking.

8.

O N THE FOURTH of July, the Steigers come to the door, and the two families walk to the high school to watch the town fireworks. It was Richard's idea and Louisa had, after a moment, agreed. Of course it would be nice to see them again. They'd bring their son, he said, and Louisa arranged her face into an expression of mild approval.

Each family brings a picnic blanket. Agatha wears neutral colors, beige linen pants and a cropped brown jacket. Her hair is loose this time, thick and silvered, one side swept back with a pin. It seems to Louisa that even the age lines around her eyes have an intentional quality, as if drawn by an expert hand. Next to her, Louisa feels callow and unfinished. At least Sylvie has brushed her own hair for once without being told. Louisa saw her standing at the hall mirror before they left, tying her hair back and untying it, brushing it again and again. Louisa had an unsteady feeling as she chose her own clothing. She opted for simplicity: a navy shirtdress and woven sandals.

The sky is still light over the field behind the high school. Just a pink ribbon wavers at the horizon. Mowed grass and insect repellent blend into a compound scent that swings open a door in Louisa's memory. Youth, anticipation. Louisa closes her eyes and pulls it in. She'd come to this field so many times as a girl to watch fireworks.

The Raders' lawn chairs sit on the wide red blanket that had once covered Louisa's bed in the city, the same blanket she'd shared with Xavier. Although it's not in perfect condition, some sentimentality has made her hold on to it. Now, a pitcher of iced tea and a bottle of chardonnay rest upon it. Richard removes a flask of brandy from his pocket and Heinrich accepts a splash into his cup of iced tea.

Gabriel lies on the Steigers' black blanket, stretched to his full length. Louisa was unnerved by the overly familiar way he'd greeted her today. He'd used her first name and smiled with such warmth, fixed his eyes upon her with such intensity, that she thought the others must have noticed. She's told no one about lending him the cabin, and now she feels trapped inside a secret with him. He luxuriates on the blanket in front of her, ankles crossed and hands beneath his head, so that his red T-shirt rides up and shows a pale band of skin. Louisa's camera is in the beach bag beside her chair, and she resists a powerful urge to take it out. It should be enough to sit in proximity to beauty, warmed by it, without appropriating it. She remembers him in this exact pose at the Pratts' party, how he'd seemed nothing but the impression of a figure then and how his solitude had stirred envy in her. This, in contrast, is a study in the commonplace. He's flanked by his parents at a wholesome family gathering. Her own daughter sits beside him in a long white sundress Louisa doesn't remember seeing before. She scans the crowd, idly twirling grass blades around her fingers.

Both Gabriel and Sylvie are quiet. Louisa tracks them in the corner of her vision as she talks with the Steigers. Sylvie is reserved tonight, but that might not carry meaning. She's always reserved. And there is, after all, an age gap with Gabriel. The years between twelve and eighteen, a chasm. They have nothing in common to talk about.

Richard had insisted on bringing the extra lawn chairs, and now Louisa is glad. There are ants in the grass, and she's pleased to offer seats to Heinrich and Agatha. Gabriel turns and looks up at Louisa. He's scooted forward so that his head is directly at her feet, making her feel uncomfortably senior.

"I've been learning about Francis Bacon," he says, as if they're continuing a conversation.

Louisa looks at him sternly.

"The artist or the philosopher?" Richard inquires, swirling his cup of iced tea.

"The artist," Gabriel says, still looking at Louisa.

"Really?" she says. "So, what do you think of his paintings?"

Gabriel smiles broadly. "They're nightmares. I love them." Agatha adjusts herself in the lawn chair.

"Also Vito Acconci and Kiki Smith and Agnes Denes," he says. "Maurizio Cattelan and Chris Burden."

Richard looks at Louisa questioningly. Neither Heinrich nor Agatha responds. It's clear their son isn't addressing them or calling on them for his art education. They sit quietly, looking toward the horizon, where the pink ribbon has deepened to plum.

"Interesting," Louisa says.

A scintillation spreads inside her, something like pride. He's teaching himself, individuating from his parents' conventional tastes. He looks up at her from the ground, only at her, waiting for her to say more, to praise him.

Children run past in glow necklaces. The members of the Nearwater marching band, a group of retirees, take their places at the end of the field. Rather than marching, they sit in chairs and play the opening strains of "The Stars and Stripes Forever." They've done this every year since Louisa was a child.

"There is nothing like this in Austria," says Agatha. "Such an American experience."

"Did you see fireworks in other towns, before you came to Nearwater?" Richard asks.

"Yes, but it still feels new to us," Agatha goes on. "Not to Gabriel, of course. He's American, after all."

Heinrich clears his throat. "He's grown up in the US, that is."

"I am American," Gabriel says. There's a touch of anger in his voice.

Richard looks at Louisa with questioning eyes. She raises her eyebrows and shrugs.

"Do you have family in Austria?" Richard ventures. Louisa appreciates this quality of her husband's, this ability to keep conversation gliding smoothly past any moguls that crop up. It's why he does so well with clients.

"Not much," Heinrich replies. "Agatha has a sister there and a brother in Germany. Otherwise, this is our family."

Agatha reaches for the wine bottle. She refills Louisa's plastic glass and then her own. Heinrich takes the bottle from her and fills glasses for Richard and himself.

Agatha takes a sip. "It is only the three of us here," she adds.

"Well, that's why it's so important to make friends," Richard announces and holds up his glass in a toast. "We're glad to get to know you."

Louisa holds up her glass, too, and the Steigers follow the gesture. Sylvie and Gabriel ignore them. They seem comfortable together. Perhaps Louisa was too quick to envision a bad episode in the basement.

"This is our favorite town so far," Heinrich says. "We like being on the coast. It is a very different feeling."

Richard nods. "I agree. It was a good change for me too. I was landlocked where I grew up and being in Manhattan felt the same way. Both were suffocating, but I never understood why until I came here."

Agatha takes another sip. "Having the sea so close, it makes me feel like there are possibilities," she says, her voice coming out a bit looser now. "As if I could swim away any time, if I wanted."

She laughs, and the Raders laugh with her. Louisa leans back and crosses her legs. It's all right to relax. She breathes deeply and thinks she detects a hint of salt in the air from the beach a mile away. She reaches for her camera. She takes off the lens cap, adjusts the f-stop, and holds it discreetly in her lap. Directly in front of her a firefly pulses for an instant, its tawdry light winking and vanishing.

She brings the camera to her eye and aims it at her daughter, who's facing away. Her pulse quickens slightly as she takes the picture, aware of being watched. Afterward, Agatha smiles at her with a glint of surprise. Louisa sweeps the camera toward her and focuses, but Agatha puts a hand in front of her face.

"She hates being photographed," Heinrich says.

"Too vain, I'm afraid," Agatha says.

"It's all right," says Louisa. She turns to Richard and snaps a quick picture. He lifts an eyebrow, the way he'd done when they first began dating, when he was skittish in front of the lens. She brings the camera down and waits.

Gabriel is looking away, purposely aloof it seems, with his arms out behind him supporting his weight. Louisa takes a breath and raises the camera to her eye. The red T-shirt drapes in the narrow space between his shoulder blades. The red is a bold stroke against the black blanket. She stares through the viewfinder a moment longer and then, in one motion, Gabriel pushes himself up and stands. He looks at Louisa, hair hanging artlessly over his forehead, and she takes the picture. He wears an expression of consternation for a moment, which shifts to a sly glimmer. Then he turns to Sylvie.

"Let's get some sparklers."

"Where do you see sparklers?" Sylvie says.

Louisa lowers the camera and nestles it back into the bag.

"There." Gabriel points. "That guy has them over there."

Sylvie scrambles to her feet, and they walk away together. Neither turns back to look at their parents.

Agatha begins to stand. Heinrich puts a hand to her arm. "Sit," he says quietly.

Agatha's face reddens slightly.

"It's all right," Heinrich murmurs. He turns to the Raders with an apologetic smile. "Agatha worries too much."

Heinrich forces a smile, takes a sip of wine.

Louisa returns the smile. "Richard's the same way."

"It's true. I do worry," Richard says. "I don't envy you, having a teenager. I dread those years. There's already so much to worry about with a twelve-year-old. Childhood isn't as simple as it used to be. There's so much more for kids to manage. There are so many ways for them to be victimized. By society and each other . . ." He trails off, looks away.

"Yes, it is a challenging time for everyone," Heinrich says.

The first few stars have taken shape above the trees, and now the sky seems to darken swiftly. The fireworks begin with a bursting green cluster, a blazing bush. The second burst is golden, a shower of coins. Although Louisa keeps her eyes trained to the sky, she's keenly aware of the surrounding field and feels unmoored amid the dim crowd. Her daughter is still somewhere out of sight—with Gabriel. The four parents sit dumbly together now, watching the light show in silence. The field is illuminated with each explosion, the huddled black forms of families suddenly blanched, like worshippers bolted to their blankets. Everyone faces east, toward the darkest part of the sky—the direction of the beach and the Sound, and beyond that, the sea.

Before Louisa sees Sylvie, she sees a flare. It moves quickly, erratically toward her. She flinches and sits back in her lawn chair.

"Did I scare you?" says Sylvie's voice.

Her daughter holds a stick with a jumping cluster of fire at its end. She moves to her father, waving the sparkler in front of his face a little too closely.

Louisa senses a presence behind her and knows without turning that Gabriel is there. Slowly, a spectrum of color descends in front of her eyes, blending from red to orange to yellow. Gabriel moves the narrow band down past her face, then settles it around her, a glow necklace. His touch is gentle and tense. She feels an involuntary shudder at the contact, followed by a warm current that spreads from the place where the necklace lands, at the top of her spine.

She remains as still as she can, letting him straighten the necklace so that it rests over her collarbones. There's an alarming intimacy in the gesture. But she reminds herself that his actions are beyond her control. He's an unpredictable boy. That's clear to everyone. And yet she's aware of her face prickling with heat. She's thankful for the darkness.

Gabriel's fingers brush Louisa's throat. Then he stands back and comes around to the front of the chair, glancing back at her before dropping onto the blanket beside Sylvie. Louisa finally moves her body for the sake of moving it, shifting in her chair, then turns and sees that Agatha is watching. Their eyes meet for a moment, and something passes between them. Louisa drops her gaze and doesn't look up again. The accusation in Agatha's expression is illusory, she knows. It, and everything else, grows from a snag that exists in Louisa's own imagination, which is the only culpable party here.

A brilliant blue fountain erupts over their heads, a thousand drops of firewater. It spreads like moonlight over the crowd. For that moment, time stops. Louisa holds her breath and takes a mental photograph, searing the image on the back of her retina. It's been a long time since she's wanted to seize an image as desperately as this. Years later, this is the moment she'll remember: the six of them on blankets and chairs, their lopsided geometry on the grass. The ecstatic blue light fades, and the fountain dries. The next flash is white and compact, a brusque rupture.

Gabriel offers a fresh sparkler to Sylvie, who sits up and takes it from him. Louisa watches as he pulls a lighter from his pocket and ignites it for her daughter. Sylvie contemplates the flare for a long moment as it jumps to life, spitting white light. Slowly, she reaches with her free hand toward the end of the stick, and her fingers hover at the corona. Louisa springs forward in her chair, and Richard yells out. Sylvie, without turning, drives the sparkler into the ground, extinguishing it.

9.

A T THE POOL, the children are in and out of the water like amphibians. Some float with arm pillows, some grip foam planks shaped like gravestones. Girls climb the diving board ladder and take turns flying into oblivion. Static among them are the mothers in their lounge chairs, empty nesters reading in the shade, and the older girls: the lifeguards and babysitters.

The boy stands outside the fence, looking in. The girl is on a towel, reading. He pings her, tells her where to look, watches as she reaches for her phone and scans the fence. When she sees him, her face brightens. She hefts the pool bag onto her shoulder and comes out through the gate. Together, they go toward the tennis courts, to the edge of the woods where they first found each other.

"You saw my message from before?" He glances at her. With her hair tucked back, the virgin earlobes are visible, unpierced.

"Yeah. I was waiting for you, but I have a book, so it's okay you were late."

"What book are you reading?"

She pulls it from her bag, a heavy science fiction novel. "It's about an asteroid threatening Earth."

"Sounds dark," he says. "I like the title." *The Instant.* She puts the book back at the bottom of the bag under her towels.

As they exit the pool enclosure, a teenage girl in a bikini comes toward them with long hair like vines, swaying her hips. The boy doesn't slow his stride.

"Hey," the older girl says to him. "I haven't seen you in a while. Are you going to Aether this weekend?"

His pace falters, and he looks at her. His eyes drop to her bare navel then travel back up. "No."

"That's too bad," she says. "It's a great lineup this year."

"It's not for me."

She slows and falls back as they walk on. Well, good seeing you."

He and the girl go in silence the rest of the way to the tennis courts.

"What's Aether?" the girl asks.

"Nothing. It's a music festival. It's supposed to be this communal, green event with art in the forest, but it's really just a corporate frat party. I went last year and hated it. It's a bunch of junk in the trees, hammocks and glitter, and T-shirts for sale in bank-sponsored tents, plastic beer cups thrown everywhere. Lots of drugs. Every year somebody dies."

They come to the boulder where the girl was sitting when the boy first saw her. She lays her towel over it. "Was that your girlfriend?"

"What? No." He shakes his head, lowers himself to the ground. There's a lost tennis ball beside him, matted by the elements. "I mean, we used to go out, kind of. Just for a little while. She wasn't that interesting or, I don't know, deep. A lot of girls change when they get older. It's like they stop thinking or caring about things."

The girl sits on the boulder, draws her legs up. "I won't stop thinking or caring."

"Good. Try not to."

"The girls my age are stupid too. All they care about is watching videos on their phones."

He lies back on the ground, among the weeds. He puts a forearm over his eyes to shield them from the sun. "That's what they're trained to do," he says. "The corporations like it when our brains are softened with entertainment. It makes us better consumers. Passive and moldable. Not knowing how to think, never mind how to rebel."

"Oh, the girls I know are definitely not rebelling."

"That's because they don't even know anything's wrong. Or if they do, they don't think there's anything they can do about it, so they don't even try. Much easier to just zone out. And that's exactly how the companies want it."

"What companies?"

He's quiet for a minute in the sun, then moves his arm away from his eyes and sits up. "Do you know who Roy Fox is?"

"I think so. Isn't he the one with all the animals?"

"That's right. I've been working for him this summer. My parents pulled some strings to get me hired there. It's supposed to be a chance for me to learn responsibility and whatnot. They thought it would be good for me because of my interest in animals." He smiles. "But Fox is an oil guy. He ran Charon Energy, the one that had the big oil spill a few years ago. You're probably too young to know about it, but it was a huge disaster, all over the news. I don't know how many animals died. You can look it up. Anyway, he resigned from Charon and he's supposed to be retired, but now he's chairman of the board of Pavo Oil. Not much better than the other one."

"I didn't know that about him."

"I didn't expect you would."

"I went to his house with my parents once when I was little. My dad did some work for him, so they took us on a tour. I remember the animals."

"So, you've been to the jail?"

"I mean, I didn't think of it as a jail back then. I didn't even notice the cages, really. I always used to love zoos."

"The animals are great," the boy says. "But they don't belong there. Fox keeps them like trophies. He's the kind of person who thinks everything is his to take. It's even worse than you think. He struts around the place with his cowboy boots and big paunch like some lord of the manor. I can barely stand looking at him."

"Why don't you quit?"

The boy doesn't respond for a minute. "I have reasons," he finally says. "And I do love the animals. I draw them during my lunch breaks. I tried taking pictures when I first started, but the staff told me to stop. Fox doesn't want any photography or recording on his property. He doesn't want anything posted or publicized. He has a reason to be private, considering all his bad press."

The boy tells her that he's always loved animals and nature. During childhood summers in Austria, when his parents were asleep at night, he'd go out the window. He'd spend hours outdoors, walking toward the mountains, then running back when they grew eyes. He imagined he was the only person on Earth when he felt the slap of cold air on his face, the ice of pure solitude. Night after night he went out until it stopped feeling like solitude. There was life everywhere: birds, deer, fish, and in the ground, slugs. There was so much sound. He pulled night air into miraculous lungs. His own body became like a friend.

"One time, when we were visiting Vienna, we went to a museum that had a grass roof and trees bursting out from the windows," he tells her. "The floor inside was all waved, like water. It was a museum for just one artist, an old man who sailed the world. He even gave himself a new name, Hundertwasser. It means 'hundred waters.'"

He tells her about the artist's paintings on the walls, bursting with mad color like paintings of the prisms in his own head. He'd looked at the paintings and wanted to cry for joy. The feeling stayed with him in church later, where he sat for hours, absorbing the silence. He stared at the stained-glass windows that shaped the light into snakes and writhing fish. Underneath everything was a concealed fire that needed containment, the passion of Christ, that glorious agony. It all meshed together for him into a divine message, a mission.

"When I think about the animals we've been painting, when I think about the ark, I think about Hundertwasser's boat, the *Regentag*, the rainy day. After the rain, after the floods sweep humans away, the animals will inherit the Earth. That's the message."

The girl nods. "It's going to be great."

"It needs to be big. We have to get people to pay attention. It needs to be big and a little scary. We have to put them off-balance, make them worry. The only time anyone else did that was a few years ago when this artist in Old Cranbury put a swarm of insects on a house. Hundreds of bugs sculpted from rubber, hand-painted. It was amazing. Flies and beetles eating this mansion, blackening it like a plague. It made the neighbors crazy. The town actually sued the guy who owned the house. The piece finally got torn down, and an antique store took some of the bugs for resale. Did you see the jewel beetle in my studio? I took it from that store."

The girl stares. "I remember it."

"I tried to do something big before, but it didn't work out. I spray-painted a mural on the high school. It took forever to make the stencil out of tag board and cut it into sections. I had to tape all the sheets together and roll them into a tube I could carry. I painted all night, but I still didn't have time to finish all the detail work."

"Do you have a picture?"

He shows her the photograph of the mural on his phone: an interpretation of *The Last Supper* with endangered animals gathered at the table, the current US president in place of the Messiah, handing out hamburgers.

"That's why I got expelled," he says, grinning.

"How did they know it was you?"

"Security cameras," he says and begins to stand.

"You never sent me the drawing you were doing in the basement that night I was at your house," the girl says. "Did you finish it?"

"Oh. Yeah. Almost. I'll send it when it's done." The boy stands and looks down at her, blinking. "So, can you come tonight?"

"I can come. What do you need me to do?"

"How about I let you splash the black paint?"

She smiles and takes her towel off the rock.

10.

A GRAY DAY with soft intimations of thunder. Louisa stands inside the sealed house and watches the workmen outside on ladders, silently washing the windows. Richard hires people obsessively. A house of this caliber must be aggressively maintained.

When her phone rings, Louisa answers in the kitchen, still within view of the workers.

"Louisa? This is Angelica."

For a moment, Louisa doesn't respond. She watches the men's legs, their boots balanced on the ladder rungs. A stream of water flows down the windowpane, distorting her view, making the legs bend sideways.

"Angelica, hello."

"I'm glad I caught you." Angelica's voice holds the sound of the city, the exhaust fumes and cocktail glasses. "First of all, I wanted to see how you're doing." She pauses. "I know you and Xavier were close once."

"I'm all right. Thank you," says Louisa, although it seems the wrong thing to say.

"We were friends all the while, you know, he and I," she says smoothly. Louisa imagines a touch of competition, of triumph, in her voice.

"I know," says Louisa.

"Well, listen. It's late notice, but I'm having a party tomorrow night and would love for you to come. Bring your husband, of course."

One of the workmen lowers himself down the ladder, and he and Louisa look at each other. His face is red and his shirt ringed with sweat. Sealed within the cool glass house, Louisa feels like a specimen.

"It's for Xavier. I know a party sounds strange, but a memorial didn't feel right, and I wanted to do something for him. I thought he'd appreciate something fun, just a group of his old friends getting together. I'm going to show some of his art."

Another flood of water cascades down the window's exterior, followed by a wide squeegee sponge. Louisa tries to absorb what Angelica is saying.

"Tomorrow night? Saturday," Louisa says.

"Come around eight, or any time after."

Louisa feels herself gripping the phone.

"Well, I think that should be fine. I'll check with Richard."

"You remember where I live?"

"Not the same place, I'm sure."

"Oh yes, I've been here twenty years, my dear."

"What was it, East Tenth?"

"Number 292. Top floor."

The men have descended now and moved out of sight, leaving their ladders behind. After Louisa hangs up the phone, Angelica's grainy voice is still in her ear. She stands and feels lightened, a kind of symmetry locking in place.

At dinner, she mentions the party to Richard but not its theme. She hopes to avoid mentioning Xavier's death to him at all. He won't come anyway.

"I didn't think you cared about those people anymore," he says.

"I don't really, but I saw Angelica at her opening, and I guess she wants to reconnect."

"I thought you never liked her."

"She seems different now," says Louisa. "I guess everyone grows up eventually."

Richard's eyes linger on hers.

"It would be an interesting change of scenery," she says.

"I'm not big on those kinds of parties. You know that."

"What kinds of parties?"

"She's still in the Village?" Richard's eyebrow twitches, and Louisa feels her cheeks warm.

"She must have a rent-controlled place or something. Maybe she owns it."

"It seems like a waste of time to me."

Louisa takes a breath. Sylvie eats her dinner, carefully ignoring her parents.

"I'm happy to go by myself," Louisa says.

"I really don't understand this fascination."

Louisa looks flatly at her husband. "It's not a fascination. I'd just like to do something different."

"It's not different by any stretch, Louisa. It's more like regression."

He bends over his plate and looks, in that moment, like an old man. She quietly stares, daring him to raise his eyes to hers. He continues to fork small, precut pieces of steak into his mouth.

The following day, she looks for something dark to wear but is drawn instead to a yellow Valentino dress in her closet, tag still attached, too interesting for any event in Nearwater. It has an accordion-pleated skirt and a high neck with small buttons. It's something she'd bought in a moment of vain excitement, but on some level perhaps she'd known her future would hold at least one more party for a dress like this.

Louisa uses a magnified table mirror to do her makeup. Just blush, mascara, and lipstick. She's never liked foundation, which seems to serve the opposite of its purpose, accentuating pores and making women look older. Now, staring at her naked skin, she notices the age spots that have appeared this summer, not freckles but faint, undisciplined splotches.

There's a new curve that bisects her cheek, echoing the smile line at her lips. It's something she might have attributed to a bad night's sleep, except that it's there every day. Still, she tells herself that a solid stretch of rest—an unbroken series of deep nights—could fill in the lines. Her skin cells just need time to knit back together, and one morning she'll wake up to find the misplaced filling restored, along with the old color and clarity. For now, she sweeps blush over her cheekbones, paints her lips wine red, and pulls mascara through her lashes. She puts a trim black jacket over the dress and leaves the house.

Eastward, toward the juvenile artists. What's so true about aging? There are those who opt against it. In a city devoid of nature, you can forget you're mortal. You can be young and fruitful, enormous forever. As Louisa walks, the hot sidewalk torches her feet and keeps her fast and alive. She sees her reflection in a window, superimposed on a couple drinking coffee. At this brisk walking pace, she's a woman in her prime, fashionable, rushed in an urban manner. The pleats of the yellow dress spread with each step. The neighborhood is different now, of course, the record stores and dive bars evolved into bistros and bridal boutiques. There's a sheen on everything. Still, her heart jumps to be here.

She'd taken so many pictures. She'd carried her camera everywhere, shooting frenetically, treating it like a lottery, hoping to hit a lucky shot. She remembers walking down this very street, following a woman in a fur coat, watching the white heeled boots kicking out from underneath, until she'd caught the moment: a boot passing over a crushed soda can glinting in the sun. Afterward, she'd lowered the camera and looked up to see an old fortuneteller in her storefront window. A young girl sat beside the woman, eating cereal. They were both watching Louisa. She'd taken that picture too. She shot pigeons, people passing in cars, the contents of trash cans, dress forms in store windows, her own reflection like a double in dark clothing. She'd wasted rolls of film, didn't bother developing some. It felt like she was battling time, catching up to those who'd come before her. There was a constant simmer in her rib cage.

She'd smoked cigarettes on the fire escape of her apartment, letting neighbors spy from across the courtyard, beneath their shared square of sky. Her darkroom was the bathroom, a towel jammed under the door. She'd plunged her hands in the tub, slipping through chemical fluid. And nights—she remembers nights in strangers' apartments, beaded curtains, a man's leather pants on the floor, a woman asleep in a bra, a fish tank with eels. A bottle of mezcal with a worm at the bottom, lipstick around the rim. The old music, raw and insistent. Iggy Pop, Joy Division. Sitting on a fuzzy toilet seat cover, watching the bathroom tiles change places. The flash of the camera quietly detonating.

She avoids the route past her old building, walking directly down Tenth Street instead, all the way to Avenue B. Kids walk heedlessly past with cordless white earbuds. But the buildings are the same, their windows and lamplight the same. These grids of windows, silhouettes of strangers living out this night in their lives. Different strangers now but equally stubborn in the insistence that they matter. They're equally aware of and oblivious to one another, preserving respect for each other's ferocious, private loves.

When Richard looks at an old city building, he sees only stain and desperation. He hadn't wanted to spend time in Louisa's apartment when they were dating; he'd insisted she come to his austere Midtown sublet. Only Xavier had ever known the way she lived in those days. She feels him hover beside her for a moment before she returns to the present, like walking into a glass pane. It's beyond comprehension that he's gone. The walls of the buildings seem to ask the same pointless questions. *Where is he? Where is everyone?* It's impossible that someone like Xavier could come and go so lightly. In and out of the world, and the cars keep driving, the bricks keep holding up buildings, the interchangeable kids keep laughing. How is there no bleeding rift down the middle of the street? The city has already regenerated itself, perfectly selfish and forgetful. Even she'd forgotten for a moment—she who'd been, for a moment, excited to go to a party.

A new shop occupies the ground floor of Angelica's building, its window displaying vintage toys: a rocking horse and a row of wooden-wheeled animals. Louisa thinks of Sylvie, feels a brief, intense spark at the memory of her daughter at home. She tries the door, but the shop is closed.

Someone buzzes her into the building, and she feels like an interloper as she climbs the four flights, hearing amplified voices in the stairwell. People are already there, with drinks. Right away, Louisa sees that this is a distinctly unmournful atmosphere. She stands in the door and recognizes no one. The apartment is much larger than the one she remembers, although she'd only been here once for some misguided reason and hadn't stayed long. No one had ever lived in a place this big back then.

Now she sees Angelica, in red as always. The silken halter top exposes her bony spine, which hunches slightly. Louisa touches her shoulder, and Angelica turns with a look of true surprise.

"You came all the way from Connecticut?"

"You didn't expect I would?"

"Well, no, not really. This is Simon."

Louisa shakes a bald man's hand, then turns back to Angelica. "What happened to the apartment? It's huge."

"What's that? Oh, you haven't been here since who knows when. I've got the whole floor now. I co-own the building with Keith."

"Keith?"

"Keith Hill." Angelica's eyes flash. "You remember him. His partner runs the little store downstairs."

The name sends a shot through Louisa. She hasn't heard it spoken in years. She latches her eyes to a brick wall adorned with a trompe l'oeil painting of a prismatic forest that seems to beckon from the other side.

"The toy shop," says Louisa.

"It does surprisingly well." Angelica takes a cigarette from the bald man, then turns back with a delayed smile. "Why don't you get yourself a drink. Everything's in the kitchen."

Louisa aims herself toward the kitchen. Already it's all happening too fast. She isn't ready to look carefully at anyone yet, not ready to recognize or fail to recognize anyone. They can just watch her for now, follow her yellow dress. Any pair of those eyes could be Keith's. She has the uncanny sense that he's there, in some corner, tracing her path to the kitchen. As she pours vodka into a cup, she keeps her gaze down, preparing to accept or deflect his approach.

He'd had yellow-blond hair back then, like pissed-on snow. His face was thin and sardonic, and his body was a bent stem, too slight to threaten anything. She'd liked him better than the other fashion photographers. He made it clear that he aspired to something more than fashion, and in this they were kindred. After he finished shooting a session with her, they'd sometimes go to Indochine and drink lychee martinis, making sarcastic remarks and winking at men. She was the only model, he claimed, he could bear talking to in street clothes.

She'd taken him to the opening of Xavier's solo show. Angelica had been there in an oxblood leather dress with zippers. Xavier held court in the corner, surrounded by paintings that still looked wet—gray planes of color like misted windows. He was taller than most of the crowd and already visibly high. Louisa sensed a change in Keith the moment the men shook hands. Later they'd all gone out, a group of six or eight, and huddled in a dark restaurant booth. They'd piled together after that into someone's car and ended the night on a roof. Xavier and Keith had vanished at some point and reappeared later with vacant eyes.

Now, Louisa takes her drink and goes back into the party. Really, there's nothing to fear, just clusters of middle-aged strangers. Intricate music is playing, an African drumbeat over atonal violins. In one corner a female mannequin poses, overseeing the room through the head of a zebra. It wears a Victorian dress with a bustle, black hooves protruding beneath. Above is a rusted chandelier fashioned from a stripped box spring. The metal grid holds light bulbs in its jaws and casts the menacing shadow of an instrument of torture.

Louisa's own apartment had been so small, the bedroom barely big enough for Xavier to stretch to full length. Houseplants had hung from doorjambs and balanced on windowsills, their leaves swooning downward, brushing the floor. There'd been little else. That place had always felt borrowed, temporary. But here's Angelica, still entrenched.

It's the home of an artist, worth a fortune now. Angelica has done it. She's gotten there. Louisa ventures forward with her cup of vodka.

A curly-haired woman lies draped on a daybed. On a nearby ottoman, a dreadlocked man tries to explain something to her, gesturing with his left hand and a glittering cuff link. The woman looks at the ceiling, her face hooked in profile, quite possibly a man. How had she known Xavier? All these people had known him and failed to save him. Here they are now, flamboyantly continuing to live and lounge and drink. And here's Louisa, too, squeezing apologetically back in, too late. Of all of them, perhaps she's failed the hardest.

Two of Xavier's paintings hang on the far wall. These from the period after Louisa, when he'd abandoned his murmuring violets and grays and turned to oversize canvases with slashes of manic, chemical color. This pair has yellow and pink bands dripping like spilled medicine. Party guests keep their distance—out of respect, perhaps, or distaste. There's something jarring, almost obscene about the paintings silently dominating the room. As if the dead artist himself has been nailed to the wall.

Louisa veers away quickly and approaches a group of framed photographs. She stares at an image for a moment before recognizing it: a young man turning to look into a vanity mirror, a Mark Morrisroe photograph, dated 1980. Mark himself is long gone. No one had saved him either.

Louisa stands near a group of women who congregate next to a cluster of David Armstrong's photographs in rococo gilt frames.

"Please," a woman with a maroon pageboy haircut is saying, "I have no use for anything natural."

"But it's not as if you can avoid it," replies a round, grayhaired woman.

"Sweetheart, I've been avoiding it for fifty years."

The gray-haired woman winks at Louisa and holds her glass up in a silent toast. The other woman rolls her eyes. A third, an Asian woman in pigtails, finishes her drink in one swallow. The Armstrong photographs loom beside them. The largest is a portrait of a man, lanky and nude, in buttery black-and-white. His eyes follow Louisa.

"But what are you afraid of? You're natural yourself. The human body."

"Ha! You flatter me."

"Look at David. Look at his boys. They're beautiful."

"I agree, and that was great for him. You're free to attempt the same. Just leave me to my evil plastics."

The gray-haired woman turns to Louisa. "Hello. And who are you?"

"Louisa Rader." She pauses. "An old friend of Angelica's."

The maroon woman looks brightly at her. "Are you an artist?"

Louisa doesn't detect sarcasm in her voice.

"I was at one point," she offers. "To an extent."

The gray-haired woman's eyebrows arch. "And you've ceased to be?"

Louisa is conscious of being taller than all these women. She tries to keep her posture straight, not to stoop for them.

"I'm in the suburbs now." She smiles. "I run an art center in Connecticut."

The women nod somberly.

"It's good that you're here," the gray woman says and toasts again.

"It's been a while," answers Louisa.

"You don't have to go back, you know. We'd never tell."

The women laugh.

"Have you seen Maria's video?"

"Maria?"

"Maria Moon. She's running it in the other room."

"She's here?"

"That's the whole point of the party, really, an excuse to see her film." The maroon woman gestures to where the artist stands outside a curtained screening room. Maria Moon is speaking demonstratively with a man, her braided hair just as long as in the pictures, touching the top of her buttocks. She wears a long shapeless dress in a color so drab it goes beyond modesty and calls attention to itself. It's the color of clay or raw canvas, an artwork not yet begun.

Louisa excuses herself to the kitchen where she adds more vodka to her cup. When she comes back out, a new group of young people has arrived, dressed in bright clothing. It seems impossible they ever knew Xavier, but then she remembers his roommates. Louisa feels newly aware of the creases in her face, the extra folds on her eyelids. She drops onto a couch by the window, near the curly-haired woman on the daybed. A thin, white-haired man in a suit strides quickly past. He doesn't meet her eyes, but she knows at once who he is. He crosses the room, leaves the party, and is gone.

Keith Hill. After the night of Xavier's opening, Keith had become too busy to visit Indochine. When she declined to move to Brooklyn with Xavier, Keith had taken her spot. She began to see Xavier less. A collector bought seven of Xavier's paintings, and she didn't see him for two weeks. The next time he came to her apartment, he fixed his bloodshot eyes on something over Louisa's head and asked how she'd feel if Keith joined them in their relationship.

"You're already friends," he said. "It would be fun for everybody."

She'd sat stunned for a moment, then stood and hit him. She'd scratched at his arms like an animal, tried to claw his face. He raised his hands to defend himself but hadn't stopped her. She'd thrashed at him until she was exhausted. Through tears, she looked at him and saw contamination. The irises of his eyes were muddled, like pools of clouded pond water. They were rimmed with red but still achingly beautiful. She'd gone into the bedroom and closed the door.

For the next hour she lay under the rumpled red blanket. She dug at the pillows, scarred with cigarette burns, where their heads had once rested. The room had a rank smell, to be expected from people who didn't clean, who had other things to think about. Why was she so angry? Would it be so strange for the three of them to love each other? She thought of the Americans in Paris, long ago, the artists she admired, their unrestricted lives. That mold was already broken. It was commonplace to live freely now. Why was she rattled when she thought of it for herself? What was it that tightened like a rivet and made her lose air?

When Xavier joined her in bed that night, she was queasy. He slid an arm over her stomach, and she flinched. She slept at the edge of the mattress, as far from him as she could. The next morning, she left. At her friend Noelle's apartment, she cried all day. When Xavier called her there, his voice was cold. She'd done him a favor by refusing, he said. She'd only been slowing him down.

Three months later, she met Richard. He dropped down gently onto her life, cooling it like rain on hot pavement.

Louisa sits quietly now and sips her drink, surrounded by broken conversation and music. Across from her, the woman still lies dramatically on the daybed. Louisa feels heavy. She remembers for a moment a feeling of jadedness, a familiar sensation of sinking into yet another couch at yet another party, the room beginning to warp. Her body weighs on the cushions, wanting to fall through the floor, through the building, all the way down to the earth.

Angelica's red torso comes into view, interrupting Louisa's descent.

"Louisa, come meet the artist."

Without thinking, she stretches her hand out to Angelica to let herself be helped up from the couch. Angelica smiles and, still holding her hand, leads her to Maria Moon. Up close, Maria is thicker and coarser than she appears in pictures. Electrified gray hairs run through her dark braid, giving it depth and dimension.

"You won't be surprised to know I'm a fan of your work," Louisa says abruptly.

"Thank you." Smoker's lines radiate from Maria's mouth, but her voice is mellow and whole. In comparison, Louisa feels like a canary.

Angelica buzzes at Maria's side, smoking her own narrow cigarette, shamelessly admiring the older woman. "Louisa has a gallery upstate," she drawls. "Or, Connecticut, rather."

"It's an art center," Louisa says. "Not very well known. But I'm hoping to get it on the map."

"I like Connecticut," says Maria. "I had a house there once, in Litchfield."

"Louisa used to live in the city, way back when," says Angelica. "She lived with Xavier for a while."

"Is that right." Maria's face changes, a barely perceptible torque.

"I took photographs for a few years," Louisa says quickly. "Nothing groundbreaking."

Maria nods, her eyes seeming to make a flash judgment. Louisa feels that she's just been indexed in Maria's mind, shelved in order of significance.

"You should come up and visit sometime," Louisa ventures.

Maria smiles patiently.

"And really, if you like Connecticut, I'd love to invite you for a residency." Beside her, Louisa notices Angelica's face fixed in a frozen grin. She goes on anyway. "The program's brand-new. You'd be the first. Your own cabin equipped however you want, on fifty acres. For however long you'd like, a week to six months. If you need an escape from the city."

"I miss Connecticut, it's true," Maria says. "I used to go up and work for a month at a time in the summer."

"I'll send you information. It would be an honor to have you."

"This summer?"

"The cabin's nearly done, so we should be ready for you."

"That sounds like something I might consider."

Angelica listens and draws on her cigarette, smirking. It occurs to Louisa that she has a life some of these people might covet. They are, for the most part, still living in sardine tins with half-dead houseplants.

"What have you been working on since I last knew you, Louisa?" asks Angelica. "I always liked your pictures, you know."

"No, I didn't know that."

"Well, it's true." Angelica smiles. "Though I might not have said it then."

"I haven't done much since, I'm afraid," Louisa says. "But sometimes I think about starting up again."

"Start, then."

Louisa looks hard at Angelica. "After all this time, please, no one cares anymore."

"Bernard would care."

"Bernard never liked my work even then. He doesn't do photography."

"But he'd find a place for it. If not, Keith could help."

Louisa is silent.

"You'd be insane to not work again. That's all. I'm just saving your life."

For a moment, Angelica looks young. The ultimatum in her eyes has lost none of its force. This is what Louisa's life could have been, living for herself alone. This is the reason people hate Angelica, of course, the only exceptions being the people in this room, who share the same focused madness.

Maria laughs. Her hair is so long, mixed with history. "Look out," she says. "I might just end up in that cabin, watching you."

The party glides late into the night. Before returning to Grand Central, Louisa walks for a long time through the East

Village, around Tompkins Square Park, down Avenue B. The bars are still open, young people pouring out, glutted and spinning. There are stories unfolding, still, all around her.

The last train has left the station. She stands in the terminal staring at the barren timetable. Stranded people curl against walls, using each other as pillows. The next train won't leave for four hours. She goes out to the street and finds a cab at rest by the curb.

"How much to Nearwater, Connecticut?"

"Two hundred for you, Cinderella." The driver winks.

She slips into the back seat and lets her body go slack as the cab moves forward, lurching each time a light turns green, until it reaches the FDR and speeds smoothly along. All at once, Louisa feels a sense of vertiginous loss. Xavier's party, his tribute, is done. She'll never see him again, this person who'd once been the core of her existence.

Late at night, they'd sometimes go to an after-hours club deep in the Lower East Side. Xavier always led the way, loose-limbed and dazzled. It was a place where the artists went at the end of the night, the beginning of morning, when everything else was closed. She remembers a barred window in the steel door, a password she'd never learned. It wasn't a place for conversation. If someone broke the taboo, if they asked, "Where are you from?" Louisa would let her eyes roll back and answer, "Here." Now she wonders how many of those girls had actually been like her: carefully bred, in disguise. How many of them had eventually married a nice man and held a bouquet of calla lilies?

Louisa speeds northward, away from the city. The dirty river drags outside the cab window. The Triborough Bridge reclines in the distance, vaunting its engineered diamonds. The sky pushes down its black helmet.

II.

DEIRDRE COMES TO work in a boatneck tunic—
something Louisa might have worn twenty years
prior—and pink eye shadow. Louisa feels a jab
of jealousy, a brainless nostalgia, before reminding herself
of the chaos of being that age. She wouldn't want to trade
places with Deirdre. But she can try to make use of her
before she goes back to college, analyze her youthful tastes,
get a read on the new generation.

"Did you hear about the golf course?" Deirdre asks.

Louisa looks at her. "What golf course?"

"Someone put animals all over the golf course at the
country club. Like, some kind of wooden totems. Look."

Deirdre holds out her phone to show a slightly pixelated
image of a green field studded with indistinct shapes situated
in pairs. In the picture, taken from afar, the field looks like
a giant strategic board game with pieces suspended in play.

"I have a friend, kind of, whose dad golfs there," Deirdre
says. "He sent this to me. He knew I'd like it."

Louisa looks closely at the image but still can't make out the shapes.

"Apparently the police are there with, like, four squad cars."

Louisa pulls back. "It must be some kind of prank. Maybe the animals are the high school mascot or something."

"But they're all different animals," says Deirdre.

"Well then, I don't know."

"I'd love to go see before they take them away."

Louisa looks at her camera. "Maybe we can," she says after a minute. "Why don't we go down there."

When they arrive, the police are on the field. One officer pulls at a sloth, dislodging the animal from the earth. A few townspeople stand by, watching. The creatures are large, between three and four feet across, cut from plywood. They've been carefully painted to represent different species, and each animal has been splashed haphazardly with black paint, which pools and drips on the grass beneath—still wet, as evidenced by the police officer's blackened hands. In the middle of the circle rests a rough-hewn wooden boat.

"Oh my God. It's even better in person," Deirdre says, taking a picture. "How did they do it?"

"Good question," Louisa says. "Maybe the boat was constructed on-site."

There's something familiar about the animals, Louisa thinks, a kind of religious angst on their faces. They look like both victims and villains, bewildered and bewildering. They remind her of something. She takes a picture.

That evening, while it's still light, she goes to the residency cabin. She hesitates before stepping through the doorway. It's cooler inside and dark. It takes a moment for her eyes to adjust. Gabriel is a dim form in the room.

"I used the saw you gave me." He smiles slightly, testing her.

"Are you in trouble now? Does anyone know it was you?"

"I don't think so."

"They're looking for whoever did it. The police."

Gabriel laughs, his eyes glittering.

Louisa burns. "You might be in trouble. And I can't be involved in this sort of thing."

Gabriel sits on a rusted stool that appears to have been fished from the sea. She looks at him, his face lit by the sun through the door. It's possible to detect the hidden men within some boys. Their faces hold the blueprint of character, some indication of the direction age will take them—the ethical worry lines in a forehead, the refinement of a jawbone, the tendency toward work or women. But Gabriel's face seems permanently fixed in the breach between boy and man, bold, precise, unrepentantly itself.

"Are you done here now?"

"With what? No, I'm not done."

"What else are you planning to do?"

"More art."

"I'll need the cabin back soon for the first resident."

"I thought I was the first resident." He stares at her, and Louisa feels pinned in his gaze, its laser blue light.

"The point is"—she breathes in—"we have an important guest artist coming next month, and I'll need the cabin back. In the meantime, try not to attract the police. Make room for the guys when they come to put in the drywall. You can submit an application this fall for a real residency, if you like." She pauses, then adds, "I understand that you're serious about this."

"Who?" he demands. "Who's the guest artist?"

"Why does it matter?"

"Tell me. I want to know."

"A New York video artist named Maria Moon."

"I've never heard of her. What's her work like?"

Louisa sighs. "It's interesting. Stark, elemental. She's been doing it for decades."

"Like Bill Viola?" Gabriel stares. He wants her to be impressed.

"No, not really," Louisa says and leaves it at that.

"But I still need this place."

"You can stay through August, but then I need to have it cleaned and fixed up."

"You don't understand." He shakes his head.

"Understand what?" she says but already feels like a traitor. "You have to go through the formal channels like everyone else. This was just a temporary favor."

It's true, she thinks. She doesn't understand. She's someone she would've hated at Gabriel's age. An adult who's after something.

"I'll see if I can find another place for you in the meantime," she hears herself say.

The boy turns away. Only a boy would do that.

She thinks of Angelica's party and Xavier and Maria Moon and remembers that she's an adult who's come through places and times this boy has never seen. She knows people who are living legends—and dead ones. Her seniority is permanent, irreversible. She's no longer a girl or a dizzy young woman.

"You didn't say what you thought of my piece," Gabriel says, still facing away.

"Pardon me?"

"You never said whether you liked it."

"Your piece? You mean the golf installation? I admit it was good. Different."

"That's all?" he says.

"Well, let's just say I'd like to see what you do next."

"I'm going to do something bigger."

Louisa notices that he's pinned sketches to the wall studs. One of them depicts a woman facing away; another, a girl's face. A third is of the cabin itself, its black shadow thrown on the grass. There's a confident fluency in them, rare for an artist so young. Louisa looks closely.

"Why are they signed *Aussteiger*?" she asks.

"That's the name I prefer. Steiger's too loaded. Also, it means 'climber' in German, and that's not me."

"No?"

"No. I'm an *Aussteiger*. Dropout, outsider. Sounds like 'house tiger.'" He smiles.

Louisa looks again at the sketch of the woman. In just a few lines he's evoked an attitude of mystery. There's something Greek about the figure, something carved and unpliable.

"Come here and look at this," he says to her softly.

Louisa steps cautiously over paint buckets and wood. Gabriel holds a book entitled *Earth Art*. He opens it to a full-page photograph, and she stands beside him to look. His head bends over the book, close to hers, and she finds herself within its halo of heat and saltwater.

"This is the Uffington White Horse in England. Have you seen it?" The page he holds open shows the white outline of a giant horse gouged into a hill. "There are white horses all over the countryside near Stonehenge and the burial mounds, but this one's prehistoric."

He flips ahead to a page that shows an aerial photograph of a green landscape.

"And this is Serpent Mound, in Ohio." A long, curving welt is visible in the earth. At one end is an oval—the head of the snake—at the other, a tightly coiled tail. "It's an effigy mound, where the ancient tribes buried their dead.

It's hardly noticeable on the ground, but look, from above it's monumental."

Gabriel continues to hold the book open, and Louisa continues to look.

"I think about these things a lot. Here were these nomadic people who lived lightly on the land but also made things like this. They literally turned their dead into a snake that lives forever. It's like a metaphor of art consuming life, of life becoming art." He's quiet for a moment. "I hate what people do to the Earth. But I also want to leave a mark." He touches the photograph in the book. "I want to make art like this."

Louisa doesn't answer. She understands. It's human nature to want to leave a stamp—and particularly the nature of artists. The urge would be at its hottest in a teenage boy.

For a long moment, they stand together looking at the book, and Louisa becomes aware of Gabriel's nearness. His breath is audible beside her, and his body contains a muffled voltage that she can feel. She shifts faintly away. He shifts in turn, keeping close. She understands that she should say something to puncture the silence, but her mind is suddenly blank. In this vacuum, the moment grows. It seems to stretch and wrap around them, and Louisa has the peculiar sense that she's returned to an earlier episode in her life, following a familiar pattern. And yet this moment, this scenario, is completely new, sharp at the edges.

Gabriel doesn't take his eyes from the page as he keeps the book open with one hand and touches her back with the other. She feels his finger touch the bone at the base of her neck and begin to travel slowly over the knobs of her spine, one by one. A long moment swells with the first touch and with each inch thereafter, as Louisa stares at the photograph, the serpentining mound. At the place where the spine curves in, he draws a jagged breath and Louisa pulls away. The book thuds to the floor.

At home, Louisa sits for a long time on the living room couch. The house is empty and cool. The workers are outside again, doing something to the bushes. When they come near the window, she stands and goes upstairs.

On an impulse, she sits on the floor in the bedroom closet and takes out her portfolios. Removing the first elasticized band, her fingers thrill slightly. She flips quickly through the pictures. There are so many she doesn't remember taking and others that are burned into her mind. Finally, she finds the photograph she wants, the black-and-white profile of Xavier, the one she sees whenever she thinks of him. He's painting, eyes aimed ahead, a slant of light across his face. He makes no sign of noticing the camera. That's how he always was while working. It's a beautiful photograph, elegiac.

The other pictures tell a disjointed story in color, a fever dream of the city. Louisa tries to remember being the kind of girl who made a record of everything, who tried to freeze the essence of people and buildings and objects, who captured the flashing details, the single moments as they clicked in place amid the whirl of activity. Complexity has always intimidated her. She's drawn to microcosm. There are pictures of strangers, parts of their bodies or pieces of clothing. There's the woman's white boot and the can on the sidewalk. There's the long-ago hem of her coat. Louisa sits on the floor and stares, her legs crossed and beginning to cramp. It's as if she's seeing the pictures for the first time. She realizes she's trying to see them as Gabriel might. It would probably surprise him to know that the young, unspoiled eye behind the viewfinder had been hers. The pictures themselves still hold a crooked beauty after all these years in their time capsule, and she's pleased to find that she isn't embarrassed by them. At some point, maybe, she'll show them to him. The idea of it excites her. She still feels the heat of his touch on her lower back.

In the hour before Richard comes home, she undresses and lies on the bed. She wants to touch her own body but resists. Instead, she puts the macro lens on her camera and shoots self-studies. Just as she used to, she zeroes in on tight details: the curve of her hip, the underside of her foot, its pink calloused landscape against the white sheets. All these years later, she crawls with self-consciousness—how had this ever felt natural?—but pushes past the feeling, past the shame at her body's sags and blotches, and becomes a simple lens, seeing only shapes and textures, clinical and defamiliarized.

When Richard appears in the doorway, she ignores his look of bemusement and asks him to hold the camera. He doesn't equivocate but takes the pictures obediently while she curls and stretches on the mattress. She feels almost like an immodest girl again.

"What are you going to do with these?" Richard asks.

"Probably nothing. Just warming up the camera," she says.

"And me too," he says.

She smiles at this rare, boyish admittance. He looks neutral as ever in his tan button-down shirt and khakis a half shade paler. He'll be leaving for Paris in the morning. A slip of emotion runs through her, a visit from earlier times, when all she'd wanted was a house, a piece of land away from the city and its deranged things, and Richard every day to herself. It's an upside-down feeling of sad relief, and of regret for his leaving tomorrow.

"Come, let's take pictures of both of us." Louisa extends her hand.

12.

THEY MEET BEHIND the tennis courts. The girl sits on the boulder in her bathing suit, and the boy sits on the ground in the scorched grass. Insects buzz in the weeds.

"Have you told your mother about me?" the boy asks.

The girl's eyes open wide, and she shakes her head.

"Okay, good. Don't."

"I won't."

There's a pause. "Has she mentioned me at all, otherwise?"

"No. What do you mean?"

The boy stares ahead at the girl's knees. "Nothing. I was just wondering."

"How was work today?" she asks after a moment. "Did you go?"

"Yeah." He looks down at the ground. His face is grim. "I'm sorry. I'm a little distracted today. I don't know if you saw the news. There's a fire in the Gulf. There was an offshore oil leak. The gas is combusting right on the surface of the waves. It looks like a volcano erupting in the ocean."

She stares. "The water's on fire?"

He looks up and meets her eyes. "Right. And I bet you can guess which company's to blame."

"Pavo?"

The boy clambers to his feet and stands in front of her, looking down at where she sits on the rock. "It's obscene. That man should be locked in a cage like his animals. He's caused enough destruction already, and even after the last oil spill, he couldn't bring himself to apologize. 'Accidents happen' is what he said. You can look it up, it's in all the news reports. 'It could have been much worse. We've done a lot of work to mitigate the problem. But accidents do happen.' He resigned eventually, but now he's back. And no one's even paying attention."

"Someone must be paying attention."

He points to her and then to himself. He shakes his head. "Look it up. Look at the pictures of the ocean on fire. And look at the pictures from the leak last time. Look at the pelicans with their wings dragging in muck. Look at the sea lions in their black coats of oil and the piles of dead fish."

The girl is quiet for a minute. "It reminds me of the book I'm reading," she says.

"The asteroid book?"

"Yeah. I mean, sort of. The kid's the only one who knows that the asteroid's coming toward Earth. He puts signs up all over the place, trying to get people's attention, but no one believes him."

"Huh. Sounds interesting."

The boy stretches his arms over his head then brings them back down. "Anyway, listen. The thing I wanted to tell you today is that I'm thinking about a new project."

He tells her about an art installation he once saw, horses tied to the walls of a gallery and another piece featuring a taxidermy horse strung from the ceiling. He mentions his recent obsession with prehistoric hill figures, especially the giant horse carved out of chalk in the ground in England.

The girl looks up at him. "Okay."

The boy tilts his face to the sky. "What I'm getting at is that I need a horse."

"A horse?"

"Just a horse." He looks back down at her.

"I can get you one."

The barn windows are still lit. The girl walks her bike into the trees and turns off the headlamp. On her phone, she looks again at the pictures he sent. The chalk horse in England, the tethered horses in the art gallery, bored, their rumps facing the center of the room.

Something like this.

He appears in a black sweater, part of the night. "It's from Austria," he tells her. "It's way too hot, but it makes me invisible."

Quietly, they walk toward the barn.

"Are there guards?" he asks.

"I'm not sure. I've never seen any."

The boy uses his weight to slide the barn door to the side. Once inside, they slink silently down the long aisles. The horses are asleep in their stalls. Only one is awake, as if waiting for them. Katherine Ramsey's horse, Excalibur. Its head hangs over the stall door, nodding up and down, a compulsive tic born from containment.

The latch is a simple metal clasp on the outside of the stall. There's a hook, too, but even a horse can lift that. Excalibur's halter hangs near the door. The girl opens the latch, and the black horse stands patiently as she fits the headpiece over its ears.

The hoof steps ring in the aisle. Neither of them speaks until they're outside, standing with the horse in the unlit parking lot.

"Are you sure you don't want a white one?" the girl asks.

"No, it has to look artificial."

They lead the horse into the trees and stop where the paint buckets are stashed. The girl tries to hold the horse still, but it pulls away at the first touch of the paintbrush. It stamps and jerks and turns in a circle. She whispers to it, strokes its neck, until at last its twitches die down. She watches as the boy gently paints the horse white, leaving a careful space around the eyes.

"Do you think we'll get in trouble?" she says.

"Not you, don't worry. If anyone asks, it was just me."

"But it's stealing, isn't it?"

"No, we're not even leaving the property."

"Well, trespassing then."

"Ha, well, it won't be my first time." He smiles at her. "You know the golf ark made it into the newspaper, right? And it's all over the internet."

"I know."

"You should be proud. You were a big part of that."

She's quiet as she watches him paint, his black hair hanging over his face as he smooths the paint over the horse's fetlocks.

"You know, the best artists are the ones who just put their work out there without being asked," he says. "If you sit around waiting for an invitation, you'll never get anywhere. The thing is to do it without asking. Once you get permission, the freshness disappears, there's no element of surprise. It's the people who spray-paint and wheat paste in the middle of the night, the ones who put their stuff in the street at Art Basel or in front of the pavilion at the Venice Biennale. Those are the ones who get noticed."

"But you want to sell your art someday, don't you? I mean, eventually?"

"Sure. But right now I can't think about that. Right now I just have to make people pay attention. I feel like I can't wait." He waves the paintbrush in the air. "The younger the messenger, the stronger the message, do you know what I'm talking about? Arthur Rimbaud was fifteen when he went to Paris. Greta Thunberg's only sixteen, crossing the ocean right now."

The girl is quiet for a minute. "What about Joan of Arc?"

"Yes!" The boy slaps the paintbrush onto the horse's flank. The white paint throws a constellation onto his sweater. "Only twelve when she had her vision. Seventeen when she went to battle."

At last, the horse's whole body is covered in creamy paint. The boy lifts a contraption from the ground, a kind of fabric hood with canisters attached. He hands it to the girl. "Can you put this on him?"

"What is it?"

"It's a World War One gas mask. I bought it online."

The mask has pockets for the horse's ears, cutout holes for the eyes. Two cans protrude from where the nostrils would be.

"Will he be able to breathe?"

"Of course. It's designed to help him breathe even when the air's toxic."

The horse lifts its muzzle, tries to pull away from the hood, but the girl holds it still long enough to insert the ears and buckle the straps. Once the mask is on, the horse shakes its head violently but finally gives up. They lead it through the trees to the paddle court, a natural gallery. There's even a moon, carved down to a rind, hanging above. Once inside, the girl unlatches the rope, drops it to the ground, and steps away. The horse walks a slow circle and breaks into a trot. It approaches the net and stops short. They watch for a long time before finally turning and leaving it there, aglow in the night.

13.

L OUISA HAS FORGOTTEN the feeling of the woods. As a girl, she sometimes explored them alone. She stepped through skunk cabbage and forded little streams that seemed to thread the ground of their own will. She came across faded beer cans and dulled bottles and assessed them like artifacts. Once, she discovered the charred remains of a campfire and a pair of stiffened underwear. She assumed teenagers, those storied creatures, were responsible for all these things.

The note she found under her windshield wiper yesterday was written in a boy's downhill scrawl. *Come to the cabin in the morning, sunrise if you can.* Now, a teenager leads her through the trees.

It's ridiculous, of course. But she'd woken before dawn without an alarm. For a few moments she'd lain tense, considering what to do. It was a shallow debate. She already knew she'd go, out of some knee-jerk curiosity, some habitual itch. If Richard were home, it might have been different.

She dressed silently in an old denim skirt and T-shirt and slipped past Sylvie's door. In the interest of quiet, she took the Tesla, started its mute ignition. Gabriel was waiting in front of the cabin. The art center lawn was rhinestoned with beads of water, and they walked across it together.

Now, as she follows him through the woods, she remembers Xavier, the club where they met, the nimbus of smoke at the ceiling, Xavier leading her through the crowd to a dark corner. Years ago, things could happen that way. She marvels at the effortlessness, so much like this feeling now in the trees.

She follows Gabriel until they come to the edge of the woods. They look out to the flat expanse beyond. There's a blush at the horizon, the glow of the sun or the city.

Gabriel stops and turns to her. "What do you think?"

Louisa scans the grounds. She sees the barn in the distance. The paddle courts are their own islands, off to the side.

"Do you see it?"

Louisa shakes her head. Gabriel points. "There."

She sees the horse. She looks at Gabriel.

"That's it," he says. "That's what I wanted you to see."

Noticing them, the horse begins to pace and snort. It tosses its head, as if to rid itself of the gas mask. Louisa feels as if she's viewing something in a dream. It hits a deep panel inside her.

"You did that?" she says.

"I just wanted you to see it. Before they take it away."

Louisa stands quietly for a moment, looking at the paddle court. It occurs to her that Gabriel must have prepared this spectacle just hours ago, that same night. She's strangely thrilled to find this surreal vision in the woods, this spectral tableau. She finds herself actively trying to absorb the moment, so unlike any other moment, until she nearly forgets who she is and where. It's the same sense she sometimes had as a young woman, that something astonishing had alit for her, just briefly, and that she must concentrate on it, memorize what she could of its beauty.

"It's haunting," she finally says. "But what does it mean?"

"It's a warning."

Louisa studies him. "Whose horse is it? Did you get permission?"

"He's a volunteer." Gabriel smiles slightly, and Louisa notices the flecks of white paint on his arms and face.

"You know horse theft is a felony."

"It's not theft, it's art. Anyway, he's not stolen, he's borrowed. Are you going to report me?"

He stands with his hands in his pockets, loosely composed. All at once, Louisa feels a deep and specific knowledge of him that stirs her. No, of course she won't report him. The horse will be found when the club opens. It will be returned, no harm done.

The low drone of a car engine comes from the distance. It's almost real morning now. She realizes her phone is still silenced. Richard might be texting from Paris, getting no reply. But this thought is abstract, untroubling. She knows this moment will vanish when the sun lifts. It will be easy enough for her to slip back into the house without waking Sylvie. Or not. She's free, after all, to float through the house or outside of it. Perhaps this moment can continue.

She pushes the thought down.

"It's getting light," Louisa says. "We should go back."

Gabriel pulls his hands from his pockets and turns. He stands for a moment. "You want to go?"

She smiles, the way an adult would. "We can't stay here all day."

He nods and takes a step into the woods, leaving the horse and the expanse of grass and the new sky behind. Louisa follows, a strange disappointment weighting her. They go through the trees until the light is sealed out, and they're in the cool dimness again.

Gabriel stops walking. He turns and looks at Louisa. As she stands, she feels a deep, hidden wave crash in her. They seem to be so far from anything now; the town itself is a faint memory, too far away to matter.

A feeling of familiarity settles in Louisa. When Gabriel comes toward her, she doesn't move. When he comes too close, she backs up and finds herself against a tree. He takes another step. There's the sense of slipping through time, detaching from the moment. Louisa feels the bark dig into her as he presses up against her, forcefully. His face is pushed against hers now and she breathes his hair. His mouth is wide and wet. He's stronger than she thought. His hands run up and down her sides, and she feels them jerk at the cloth of her skirt. Like a teenager. A tiny siren blares in the depth of her brain, muffled out by the sound of his breathing. She's in another place now, another time, and she's a teenager too. He pauses for a moment, shuffling at the fabric between them. Her hands move to his, guiding them. Then he takes one more step, impossibly, toward her. Into her. She gasps and fuses to the tree.

Afterward, she knows nothing but those eyes, blue like the beginning of time. Her skin is exquisitely numb. But there's something else beneath the numbness. Something hard and tangled, an egg with a broken bird inside it.

The boy opens his mouth and moves it to speak, but there's no sound. He swallows and tries again. Louisa puts a hand quickly over his mouth and shakes her head. For a moment, his wet lips relax into her palm. Then he jerks away and stares, his face flushed.

"I think—"

"No," she says.

He comes in for a kiss, and she pushes him by the shoulders. He stumbles back. His red shirt is patched with sweat, his hair pasted to his forehead. He appears to Louisa, then, as a small figure at the end of a tunnel. She feels the dark walls begin to cave in toward her. He turns away and half runs, half rambles into the woods.

Louisa stays a few moments longer, leaning against the tree. Above, the leaves frame diamonds of brightening sky. Before she's conceived of it as a decision, she begins to walk. The fact of Richard's existence is lodged somewhere inside her, buried beneath polychrome layers of sensation. She hasn't yet resurfaced in the present moment, remembered who and where she is. She's thirty-nine, twenty-nine, nineteen. She walks without thinking, negotiating tree trunks and brambles, a mindless being operating on instinct.

At last, she comes out of the woods onto an unfamiliar road. The only house in sight is a brick colonial she doesn't recognize. She walks past it along a row of clipped hedges. The next house is stone, set back from the road. The hum of a car approaches and she edges onto the grassy shoulder. The car gives her a wide berth, crossing into the other lane, and she straightens her posture as she walks, loosening her arms so that they swing at her sides with something like purpose. She's a woman out for a morning stroll. She tries to believe this as she walks past house after house until she comes to the end of the road. A street sign is there, half-hidden by a tree branch. Arrowhead Road. She's gone farther than she thought.

When Louisa finds her car and reaches her own driveway, she pauses. The small bird twists inside her. Another part of her brain takes control, begins to devise an explanation for herself in case Sylvie is awake. An early morning errand is out of character but will have to suffice. She avoids the front door, walks around the back of the house, and enters the unlocked screen porch. There's no sound indoors that she can discern. In the living room, she lies on the couch, her heart drumming in her ears. She tries to breathe slowly, gazing out at the wide lawn and the rough trees beyond.

14.

A POLICE REPORT appears in the newspaper that week:

A horse was taken from its stall in the Nearwater Hunt Club on Tuesday evening and found on the grounds Wednesday morning. Police are investigating and urge anyone with information about this incident to contact the station.

Not mentioned in the report is the fact that the horse was cloaked in white paint and caged in a paddle court, wearing a gas mask. Deirdre describes those details to Louisa, shows her the pictures on her own camera.

"My friend saw it first," Deirdre says, "and called me right before the police came."

Louisa feels a jolt. She looks at Deirdre searchingly. "Your friend really has his finger on the pulse."

"Well." Deirdre blushes. "He plays paddle tennis with his dad every morning, pretty early."

Louisa is quiet for a moment, waiting for Deirdre to give a hint as to what else she or her friend might have noticed, what else hadn't been mentioned in the report. She takes a slow breath. Of course, neither Deirdre nor her friend could have seen into the woods.

"Well," Louisa says thinly. "What did you think of it?"

"What?"

Louisa gestures to the picture on the screen.

"The horse?" Deirdre looks at Louisa. "I don't know. The whole thing's totally bizarre, especially since it was stolen."

Louisa nods. She's been spilling over with a kind of frayed electrical energy. Her heartbeat won't slow down, and she feels the tangled bird still trapped inside her. She looks again at the camera screen. The image is arresting, the horse's head in its hooded mask, stretched down to the baseline of the court. From a distance, it appears to be bowing to something. As she looks at the picture, she feels the start of a hollow burn. She smells the damp leaves again. She feels the tree bark, the push of the boy's ribs against her.

"Have you had any more RSVPs for the gala?" Louisa asks Deirdre.

"Just a few. I think we're up to forty. Everyone's away now, though."

Louisa nods. She already dislikes the gala, although she'd been the one to suggest it to the board. It shouldn't have surprised her that Carol Christensen had pounced on the idea, famous as she is for her glamorous parties on Pelican Point. As chairman of the board, Carol's husband had been the one to bankroll Richard's renovation—the Christensen name is etched over the door to the gallery—and so the gala would have to be spectacular. Louisa has forgotten how much she hates details, and planning a formal event is nothing if not a celebration of detailed frivolity. There are hundreds of miniscule decisions to be made, from hors d'oeuvres to centerpiece arrangements to video projections to the pricing of tables. The volunteer committee is cacophonous in its monthly meetings, everyone talking over each other, full of outlandishly stupid ideas. Louisa's blood pressure rises as she puts on a serene smile and nods, thinking to herself, *Never again*. She's delegated everything she can to Leigh, the grant writer, despite her steep hourly rate. Leigh has done the menu tastings with the caterer, ordered the flowers, chosen the table settings. Leigh has rented the tent and decided whether to go with the ballroom chairs or something more modern. Louisa had managed to avoid all of this hand-wringing in her own small wedding—the only event she'd ever planned—and can't bring herself to care.

"Here's another one that just came in," Deirdre says, looking at her computer screen. "Steiger. Heinrich and Agatha."

The lurch in Louisa's stomach is so strong that she trembles. She gives Deirdre no response. It isn't shocking that the Steigers have accepted her invitation. But the sound of the name alone sends her back into the woods. She closes her eyes for a moment and opens them again before she can see his face. As long as she keeps her eyes open, she'll be fine. She can pretend nothing has happened. Already the scene in the woods carries the feeling of a dark childhood fantasy. It isn't exactly real, doesn't have to be real. Its actions are the actions of a dream that don't count toward the record of waking life. They register only on another plane, untied to this one. Everyone operates on two planes: this sunlit plane of galas and husbands and daughters, and the other shadowed plane that runs parallel and never meets it, never impacts the logic of day. The second plane can't be controlled or accounted for, any more than dreams can—or art. She must relegate everything—the woods, the horse, the boy—to that dream plane. If she's going to survive, Louisa understands that she can never revisit them there.

The next moment, she hears footsteps crossing the gallery, and Gabriel is standing in the doorway as if summoned. There's a rabid look in his eyes.

"Can I see you outside?" he says to Louisa.

A vibration travels along her skin and her lips feel suddenly numb. "I'm sorry?" she answers.

"I need to see you."

Louisa glances back at Deirdre, who sits mutely at her computer. She knows she has to say or do something. A roaring begins in her ears. She thinks of taking him outside, gripping and shaking him, sending him away, but even following him out of the room would be suspect. And she's afraid of what might happen if she does.

"All right. If you won't come outside, we can talk here."

Louisa's heart trips in hard syncopation. "Gabriel."

"I just want to talk," he says in a lower, meaningful tone. "I have an idea for a show."

The roaring in her ears is so loud that his words seem to reach her through a long-distance transmitter. He says something about floods, filling the gallery with water, sailing animals on a raft.

"I just need to find a good sealant to make the craft watertight," he says.

He pauses. There's a short interval of quiet and clarity between them, and she momentarily forgets about Deirdre. His eyes lock on hers. The wave she'd felt in the woods rises in her again, threatening to crest.

She looks away.

"No, I'm sorry," she says. "There's no way the board would go for your idea and neither would I. In any case, I think that for now you'd be better off with more conventional output. You should be working on building your portfolio, showing your actual skill instead of trying to shock people."

"But what's wrong with shock? Isn't that what good art's supposed to do?"

"Not here," she says. "I'd think you'd have learned that by now."

She turns back to her desk. Gabriel looms behind her. She can feel him there. Deirdre peers intently into her computer screen.

"I should have known what you'd say." Louisa hears a change in his voice. It quavers with the petulance of a disappointed child. She doesn't turn around but instead pretends to sort through the stack of magazines on her desk. "I think it's ironic you don't want projects that shock. Especially after our project in the woods."

Louisa's hands pause, shuffling the magazines. Deirdre types something loudly, trying to seem occupied.

"But never mind. If you won't help me, I'll find someone who will. It won't be hard. There are plenty of people who'd want to help. I know Sylvie would."

Louisa spins toward him. "What are you talking about?"

"I'm just saying that I have friends who can help. I have people who understand what I'm trying to do and who want to be part of it. You'll see."

"What does Sylvie have to do with anything?"

"Why don't you ask her?"

"She's not your friend," Louisa says, hearing the gravel in her voice. "She's twelve."

"So? How do you know she's not my friend?"

"When do you ever see her?"

"I see her at the pool sometimes."

The look he gives her seems to carry a suggestion. Louisa's head feels light. "I think you need to leave now."

"All right, but you're making a mistake." His voice is softer. "Don't worry, I'll figure it out on my own."

"I'm not worried," she says as he goes out the door. Louisa hears his steps retreat over the gallery floor. It's quiet in the office for a moment.

Finally, Deirdre says, "Who the hell was that? Was that the same kid who wanted a gallery show before?"

Louisa's hands shake, and she takes a few breaths before speaking. "That's right." She tries to laugh. "He thinks he's the Michelangelo of Nearwater." She lifts the oldest issues of *ARTnews* from her desk and drops them into the recycling bin.

15.

L OUISA HAS BEEN in the habit of dropping Sylvie off
at the pool for diving practice, but today she accom-
panies her. "I haven't watched you dive all summer,"
she says, and Sylvie gives her a questioning look. "What?"
Louisa says. "Other moms watch, don't they?"

"Yeah, but they're annoying."

"I promise not to be annoying."

When Sylvie was first learning to dive, Louisa had cheered
her on. Sylvie had asked her mother to score each of her
attempts between one and ten, and Louisa had never given
her any score below seven. For years before that, Sylvie had
insisted that her mother join her in the shallow end to play
Marco Polo. Louisa knew it was hard to be without siblings,
the built-in playmates other children had, so she often agreed
to stand in. But there'd been times when she was too tired or
cold to go in the water. There'd been times she was exasperated with Sylvie, who instead of playing with other children
at the pool, demanded that she and her mother pretend to

be dolphins. Now, as Sylvie walks through the pool gate far ahead of her, she finds herself wishing for one more chance.

She finds a pool chair away from the others, in the corner of the grass near the diving boards, and hides behind her sunglasses and book, dissuading anyone from approaching. She doesn't want to engage in summer small talk: what other mothers' children are doing for camp this year, where their families are going on vacation. She's too tense for this. She's here as a spectator but also as a guard. Every few moments she looks up and scans the pool area. She looks beyond the fence, tries to see into the trees. There's a darkened patch way off near the tennis courts that might conceal a figure, but it never moves or changes. Just a pocket of shadow.

She tries to relax, to appreciate the perfect day, the cobalt sky and its small village of clouds, clean and white as the very first clouds. Sinking into the pool chair, she feels the pull of lethargy from a bad night's sleep. She tries to read her book but can't get past the second sentence. She keeps glancing at Sylvie, who sits at the pool edge, apart from the other girls, waiting her turn on the diving board. Her legs dangle over the side, and she stares fixedly at the water, seeming to watch the lane lines shimmy on the floor of the pool. Each time a diver breaks through the water, the lines fracture and dance back together.

When the coach calls her name, Sylvie snaps up to join the line for the board. Louisa watches her climb the ladder. Her bathing suit shows the beginning swells of hips and breasts.

Sylvie stands for a moment at the base of the board, gathering herself, then takes three long strides and springs. The dive turns into a flip, and she becomes a blur of color—skin, swimsuit, skin—suspended in air. Everything that makes up Louisa's child is inside that tight ball. Then the splash, and her body is gone. The water's surface tears apart and rushes to mend itself. Louisa finds that she's holding her breath along with her daughter underwater. Together, they glide. Then the urgency, the reflexive push to the surface. Together, they touch the side of the pool and slide up for air. They open their eyes, and the sky and trees and people return.

As diving practice grinds on, three other girls settle on towels near Louisa. At first, she assumes they're teenagers, but with a second glance she recognizes them—girls in Sylvie's class. It seems impossible that their transformation could be so drastic. One of them sucks on a tongue of hard red candy. The bottom half of her hair has been bleached and dyed purple. She wears a triangle bikini, already filled out. Her dangling earrings match her gold glitter phone case. All three girls are in similar bikinis, all three lost in their shining phones. From time to time they look up and laugh about something. They don't seem to register who Louisa is, for which she's glad. She's never been a fixture at the schools like some PTA women. To these girls, she's just a lady with a book. She's close enough to hear snippets of their conversation. One of them is saying something about her ex-boyfriend, who's now with someone else.

"That skank."

"He'll ditch her too."

When did this happen? When had these girls, whom Louisa remembers as toddlers splashing in the wading pool, become vixens? Which of them would be the first to send a nude photo to a stranger, if they hadn't already? Are their mothers and fathers asleep, like Richard's client had been? Louisa looks at Sylvie, sitting alone at the edge of the pool again, lost in her dreamworld. Physically, socially, she's far behind these girls. Louisa shivers in the sun when she remembers the suggestive look Gabriel had given her.

She watches her daughter appear on the diving board and feels a crazy urge to run and pull her back down the ladder, to put her in the car and drive home. As Sylvie stands and prepares herself, the coach watches. The other team members watch, the bikini girls watch, everyone at the pool watches, and whoever might be in the woods. In the spotlight of their collective gaze, Sylvie steps forward and launches into the air.

Later, after Sylvie is safely in bed, Louisa leaves the house quietly. The night is fully dark as she pulls into the art center driveway and parks with the headlights aimed over the field. She walks in their beams until she reaches the forest and goes the rest of the way with a flashlight. There's a premature bite in the air, and she crosses her arms over her chest as she approaches. Her mind is vacant, no script planned. All this time, she's been firmly encased in her daytime world. As long as she didn't pierce its membrane, she thought she'd be safe. Why had she assumed that this boy would do the same, that he'd stay locked in his box in the trees? Now, she's here and he has to go.

When they'd come out to the car after diving practice, Louisa had found a piece of folded paper under her windshield wiper. Unfolding it just slightly, she'd glimpsed what it was. She'd deflected Sylvie's questions, told her it was an advertising flyer, not worth sharing. As they got into the hot car, she'd made a show of blasting the air conditioner while shoving the drawing into the depths of her purse. It was a startling likeness. He'd even replicated the angled pockets and single button of the white suit she'd been wearing that first night at the Steigers'.

A dim light shines through the cabin window. She knocks at the door and opens it without waiting. There's a new table in the corner, lit by a desk lamp. A woman sits bent over the table, a long gray braid down her back. She turns to Louisa and, upon recognizing her, smiles widely.

"Louisa, I wondered where you'd been."

Maria Moon, now standing upright beneath the low ceiling of the cabin, appears somehow larger than she'd been in Angelica's apartment—and younger. She's a week early; Deirdre must have welcomed her in Louisa's absence. To Louisa's relief, someone has put in a mini fridge and plugged in another floor lamp. The only evidence of Gabriel's time here is the rusted stool and a painting on the brand-new drywall, a weird four-legged creature with a human face.

"I like the animal here," says Maria, gesturing to it.

"A local artist did that for us," Louisa improvises.

She sees that Maria has already colonized the other walls with glossy video stills. A desktop computer and other sleek machines are plugged into a power strip. Maria crouches and lifts the strip in her hands. There's a low whirr of electricity.

"Do you have another of these? I should have brought two."

"I'll check," says Louisa. "Do you have everything else you need?"

"Yes, absolutely, Louisa. And thank you for inviting me here. Really. I think it will be a good escape."

"We're honored to have you. Work well and let us know if we can help."

Back in the car, Louisa feels strangely abandoned. She still sees the creature's eye looking out from the wall. And, as she drives, she feels the eyes of the houses on her, alert behind their moats of floodlit shrubs.

16.

AFTER SEVERAL WEEKS without rainfall, drought conditions are declared in Nearwater and throughout the Northeast. The Connecticut sky is white, swollen, full of vapor that won't condense. The flamingo pond shrinks at the Fox estate. The property's hundred acres sprawl at the northern edge of town, where the roads turn to dirt, where the ultrarich hide. The stone house itself, ten thousand square feet, is styled as an English Tudor, a citadel on a hill. The new cedar addition juts from its side, sleek and slanted. The property is divided into vast enclosures for the animals, divided by species. No expense has been spared on the outbuildings, the staff building, the storage sheds. Richard Rader has brought the whole vision to life. The front gate is a folly of Fox's own invention: ornate iron hatchwork topped with elephant heads. On either side are plaques with Bible quotes:

The wolf will live with the lamb, the leopard will lie down with the goat, the calf and the lion and the yearling together; and a little child will lead them.

Be fruitful and multiply. Have dominion over the fish of the sea and over the birds of the air and over every living thing that moves upon the earth.

The staff of five tends to the landscaping, does maintenance, and travels to the animal enclosures in golf carts. They toss food for the Caribbean flamingos: pellets containing shellfish that turn feathers pink. They give chicken legs to the African servals, they feed the kudus, the red pandas, the kinkajous and camels. The golden lion tamarins chatter overhead in an allée of tamarind trees.

Today, the girl arrives at the gate on her bicycle, wearing riding boots and jodhpurs. The boy waits to greet her. He pushes the button that makes the gates swing open, and she pedals beneath the gaze of the iron elephants.

"I'm supposed to be riding all day," she tells him with a grin.

"Good. I want to give you the full insider's tour."

Together, they visit the flamingoes that mince in the stagnant pond and the camels that languish in a dusty pen. They watch the orange tamarins scuttling in the trees, screaming bloody murder.

"How does he know if they're happy?" the girl asks quietly.

"That's not a big consideration, I'm afraid," the boy says.

They watch the kudus, grazing in their grass pasture.

"They're beautiful, aren't they?" the boy whispers. "Sometimes I think maybe it's better they've never known freedom.

They don't even know they're wild. And they're safer here than kudus in Africa. There are no predators, and they have all the food and water they need. A vet even comes to check up on them."

One of the animals lifts its head with its delicate nostrils and ears, its proud corkscrew horns.

"Do you really think they're better off here?" the girl asks.

"No."

They go over the grass to the next enclosure, where the giant anteater comes rambling out of its hut. Its backside and front are symmetrical, its thick hind legs carpeted with fur, a white racing stripe on its haunch. It glides toward its dish of insect gruel and laps it up with a sharp lash of tongue.

"In the wild, it pulls food right out of the ground with its snout," the boy says. "No other animal does that. It just takes what it needs from wherever it's standing. It comes out to eat during the day, but it's mostly nocturnal. I snuck in to visit at night once so I could watch it. There's a loose slat in the fence behind the enclosure, and there's no security here, believe it or not." He's quiet for a minute, watching. "This species is twenty-five million years old."

"And now it's alone in a cage," the girl says.

They move to the next enclosure and stop outside the chain-link fence. Two African servals pace at the far end of their enclosure among scrubby bushes meant to replicate the savannah.

"It was one of these wildcats that clawed that kindergart-
ner, I remember," the girl says. "It reached right through the
chain-link fence and clawed through her shirt."

The boy nods. "They're gorgeous, but they're vicious."

They watch the servals in silence. The cats are long legged
and limber, with oversize ears like bats. There's a charge in
their movements, a wound-up vitality, a shock of intelligence
in their eyes, as if they'd rip apart the fence if they could.

The boy touches the girl on the shoulder. "Look," he
whispers. "Here he comes."

Roy Fox is striding down the hill from his mansion. He's
not a tall man, and he looks older in person than in the pictures online, his hair half-gone. He wears a chambray shirt
and clean dark-blue jeans. His boots are made of reptile
skin with silver toecaps.

"Well, aren't you just the sweetest thing," he says to the
girl, then looks at the boy. "Is this your sister?"

"Yes," the girl answers for him.

"Well, she's a real dumpling. You take her wherever she
wants to go. Give her the royal tour. Just don't get too close
to the fence, remember? These cats have long arms." Fox
smiles. He has weak blue eyes with specks of pepper. "Oh,
and I got some good news today. Tell Diego, he'll be happy.
I heard back from my contact in Amazonas and he's got a
lead on some two-toed sloths. There's a family rescued from
the fires that's in decent shape and I'm gonna make an offer.
The shipping will probably be more than the price itself."

He winks at the girl. "How'd you like to see some sloths, honey? They're awfully cute."

"That's great news," the boy says.

The girl says nothing. Her gaze travels over the man's belly, soft and wide in front of her. A silver belt buckle is engraved with his initials.

As the man goes back up the hill to the house, the boy and girl are quiet for a moment. When he's out of sight, the girl says, "Was he talking about the rainforest fires?"

The boy's eyes linger on the hill where the man vanished. "Yes, he was. When he's not stealing oil, he's stealing animals. And he's ordering these guys around to trim his imported trees and spray toxic chemicals." The boy's voice rises as he gestures to a golf cart crossing the property. "All these ugly little buggies powered by little tanks of gas. He's not worried about any of it. Not the fires, not the rainforest ecosystem, not the global temperature rise. Not the tankers of oil or the private planes or the methane farts or the dead fish on beaches."

The boy has begun walking, his pace increasing as he talks. The girl trots to keep up with him. They cover the wide acreage on foot until they come at last to the tiger. The creature naps in the shade, its body flat against the bare ground. It rises as they approach. When the boy thrusts a skewer into a bucket of raw beef, the tiger stalks close to the fence, and they can see the markings on its face, the fevered brushwork. The broad bridge of the nose, the gold eyes, the barbed pupils. The tiger rocks back and forth, grumbling. When the boy holds up the skewered mass of flesh and tendon, the tiger's grumble becomes a roar. He lets the tiger have the beef and feeds it the rest, piece by piece from the bucket. The last, largest hunk he throws over the fence. The tiger lifts the meat in its beautiful mouth and strides away, moving like liquid.

"Amazing, isn't it."

The girl nods, unsmiling.

They return in the golf cart to the staff building, where the other workers have congregated for lunch. There's a smell of deli meat and mustard. They fawn over the girl. It's so rare to have visitors. They miss the school field trips. She's like fresh air. *Which animal is your favorite?* they ask.

The space is jumbled with buckets and brooms, gas cans and lawn mowers. There are huge sacks of pellets and feed, jugs of weed killer and pesticide. Keys hang arrayed on a pegboard, everything carefully labeled.

"Everything we need to run the place is right here," the boy says to the girl in a weirdly theatrical voice. "All the equipment, all the keys to the animal enclosures. Mr. Fox trusts us with his treasures. It's a lot of responsibility, but it's also a great privilege." He looks at the men. "Don't you agree?"

The men nod and laugh with their mouths full. The boy turns to the girl and smiles.

17.

THE END OF August, Sunday. Louisa makes pancakes, some thousandth family breakfast. Richard stacks and butters his before cutting them into a grid, as is his habit. Sylvie slowly makes her way through a single pancake. Louisa tries to concentrate on her own movements, one after another. The only safe place is in the moment. If she wanders from it, she'll begin to think of all the mornings behind them and the mornings in front. Before long, Sylvie's chair will be empty. And one morning, on the calendar of some unknown year, she and Richard will share their final breakfast together.

It's cool in the house, the way Richard likes it, but outside the heat is heavy. The trees are deep green now, their leaves beginning to dry and brush together in whispered discussion of the coming change, the imminent end of the season. Each year it seems impossible that such expansive, generous life should be defeated. The temperature is still high. Each day still promises the crass leisures of summer.

Louisa fights against the grinding, restless feeling that makes it hard to sit still in her chair. The sounds of her family chewing are intolerable. She supposes this is understandable. They haven't gone anywhere in months. The rest of Nearwater is away in Cape Cod, Maine, Europe, but Richard is beginning a new commission and Louisa is feeling urgency about the gala. She knows she wouldn't be able to relax anywhere. They'll take a trip after the gala, maybe the long weekend at the end of September.

For now, she'll try to absorb these last summer days. Sylvie will be starting school in just over a week. She has only a sliver of childhood left. Already she's begun the process of steady, permanent distancing. She doesn't call for Louisa at night anymore when she can't sleep. She just stays in bed alone. This is something to be pleased about, of course, that her daughter is using coping strategies, practicing autonomy. It's healthy to have air between them. Still, Louisa envies mothers with younger daughters who seem to share a common language, who still have an easy physical intimacy. She feels that she's been shortchanged in this respect. Sylvie was a fussy baby who'd resisted being held, who hadn't wanted to nurse, who'd twisted out of her mother's arms. The closeness between them had spanned only a few years. In truth, Sylvie was rarely demonstrative with anyone. Her young friendships had always been somewhat remote. There were none of the alliances that were like love affairs between other girls. Her teachers reported that she spent recess time alone, playing beneath the trees, planting acorns in the ground. Even now, she doesn't belong to any of the social cliques that have rapidly formed. The girls she sees most are from the hunt club, from different schools, but she doesn't invite them to the house, and they don't invite her.

Sylvie is clearly her father's daughter—independent, internal, and equally opaque. The two of them can sit quietly together for hours. He's begun teaching her to play chess, the mere idea of which is miserable to Louisa. She's been struck by her daughter's swift grasp of strategy, how she sits at the white Tulip Table with her father, leg tucked beneath her, engrossed in the cryptic pattern on the board. She's also begun playing the guitar again, having abandoned lessons years ago. These days, sitting on the floor with her guitar, hair lightened by the sun, Sylvie looks like a girl from the past, an ardent flower child. Watching her daughter pick out melodies, stopping and starting again, Louisa marvels at her new tenacity. Or maybe it was always there. She remembers Sylvie's preschool obsession with ants, how she'd spend hours watching them and helping them cross the driveway on leaves like magic carpets. She'd go out every day to do this, sitting with the focus and patience of a tiny Jane Goodall.

Now she's begun asking to stay home alone when Louisa and Richard go out. Other kids are at sleepaway camp, she argues. The least they can do is allow her this breath of freedom. Louisa has consistently refused, but Sylvie's persistence has been wearing her down. *Maybe we can try it soon, for just a short time,* she's finally relented. *We'll see.*

"The Foxes are coming to the gala, by the way," Louisa tells Richard at the breakfast table.

"Really? I'm surprised."

"I know. I didn't think they were into art either. Whenever I mention the center to Marilyn, her eyes go dead."

"They're probably amping up the philanthropy right now because of the pipeline leak. It's all about PR."

"What's PR?" Sylvie asks.

"Public relations," Louisa answers. "Trying to control the way people view a company. Pavo Oil has had some problems, and Mr. Fox is the head of its board of directors. Anyway"—she turns to Richard—"you're probably right. They bankrolled the whole children's hospital after the first spill. Marilyn's a genius with this stuff. Roy would've been run out on a rail without her."

"The children's hospital where Katherine died?"

Both Louisa and Richard look at Sylvie. "Yes," Louisa says. "It's the only one around here."

Sylvie doesn't say anything else and instead returns to her pancakes.

As they clear the breakfast dishes from the table, distant thunder sounds. It hasn't rained in weeks. Outside the windows, the world has a hazy matte quality. To Louisa, there's something compelling about the complete lack of shadow or depth, this general flattening, like a color-field painting.

Sylvie disappears into her room and Richard into his office. Louisa goes upstairs for her camera and stops at Sylvie's bedroom door to listen. No sound is audible, no turning of pages. She's probably looking at her phone. Louisa touches the door but chooses not to knock.

Back downstairs, she stops at the living room window and frames the green sweep in her camera's viewfinder. Focusing, she stares and waits for the moment of enchantment. As she presses the shutter, she becomes aware of appraising the image through Gabriel's eyes.

She lowers the camera and evaluates the picture in the display screen. It's bland, unimpressive, failing to convey the gradations she sees, the ominous quality of light. She's embarrassed by her pretentious attempt at minimalism and cringes to think how someone like Gabriel might criticize it. Is this the best she can do, photographing her own property, land she's done nothing to earn? She turns the camera off and puts it down. A wave of sickness comes through her. Somehow, she's let this boy break out of the compartment in her mind. When he came to her in the office, she'd seized up. He must think she's ridiculous, a middle-aged woman pretending to be a girl. A weak conquest for him, the beginning of a long line of conquests. When she refused to accommodate him, she heard the scorn in his voice. He'd seen how helpless she was, how useless. The sickness roils her stomach as she remembers this. Why had he mentioned Sylvie at that moment?

The thunder rumbles a warning. Despite the coming storm, she needs to leave the house. When she tells Richard she'll be out for a couple of hours, he glances up from his book and says, "Be careful."

The first fat drops of rain explode on the windshield and pound the roof as she drives. The wipers can't clear the thick glaze. She runs through the parking lot into Neiman Marcus, feeling the excitement of entering the building with soaking clothes and hair, all alone. The store is nearly empty, and she breathes in its scent of perfumed luxury. She's decided to allow herself this one indulgence: a new designer ensemble for the gala. This isn't just a party, it's *her* party. As director, she'll be the center of attention. If there was ever a time to let her personal style come through—all the fashion sense she's stored up for years with no outlet—it's now. She can't just wear a corporate pantsuit or the kind of high-ruffled cocktail dress favored by women in town. She needs to be her own piece of art.

After an hour of rifling through the racks, she finds an embellished Dolce and Gabbana corset. The mosaic of candy-colored jewels hides only some of the corset's boning, so that it straddles the line between class and scandal. The two-thousand-dollar price tag can be mitigated by wearing simple black satin cigarette pants and heels she already owns. The angled mirror exaggerates her slender height, and for the first time in years she loves her reflection. Quickly, before she can let herself judge through a boy's eyes, she turns away and undresses. She pays and goes outside with the garment bag. It's already stopped raining. The sun has broken through, and the parking lot asphalt steams. She slides into the Tesla and feels the rush of driving home with something beautiful.

She stops at the mailbox, brings the stack of worthless mailers inside to be recycled. Sorting through them at the kitchen counter, she finds an envelope, plain white with no stamp or address. She slices it open with a fingernail and pulls out a sheet of heavy paper. It unfolds to reveal a drawing of a woman, unclothed. The lines are dark and sure, and it takes only an instant to recognize herself.

18.

F ROM THE OUTSIDE, the glass house blazes. Indoors, it's a cold white museum. The girl is home alone, in her bedroom, gazing into her phone. A video plays: footage of fire in the ocean, an eye of boiling magma. The girl watches, then closes the tab and drops the phone on the bedspread. She lies on the rolling fabric of stars, and with a finger she traces the shape of a tiger.

When a noise comes from downstairs, she sits up. The sound comes again, a knocking, and she quietly slides off the bed and pads down the hallway with bare feet. At the top of the stairs, she listens. The knocking repeats. She moves down the stairs slowly, with shallow breaths, hesitating at each step. Halfway down, a shape comes into view outside the sliding glass door. She stops. A fist thumps on the glass. A face appears.

As she descends the rest of the stairs, their eyes meet. She breathes normally again. The boy looks past her, as if searching for something. She glances behind her, then back at him. She pulls the door handle, and the glass sighs open.

"What are you doing here?" she asks.

"Is your mother home?"

"No. Why?"

The boy doesn't answer. His Adam's apple shifts up and down. He looks past her again, and his eyes skim the living room.

"Are you looking for her?" she asks.

"No." He shakes his head hard, as if chasing away a fly. "No," he says again. "Just you."

19.

THE DAY IS too beautiful for work. The world is gilded with the dry sun of late summer, trees rustling their mature leaves like taffeta. There won't be many more of these days. There are only a few of them in any year, any lifetime. Louisa feels no guilt about spurning the office to play tennis with Kelly Pratt.

Each time her racquet makes contact with the ball, a dart of satisfaction lights up part of her brain. As she prepares her serve, squinting against the sun, an idea comes to her. She'll spend the next week editing and printing her new photographs, and she'll choose one to donate to the gala auction. Rather than tying her own name to it, she'll contribute anonymously and leave the print unsigned. Let collectors consider it on its own merits and bid what they think it's worth. Afterward—depending on whether the piece sells, and for how much—she'll reveal herself as the artist. They'll be surprised, delighted. They'll be impressed with her modesty, having performed the role of arts administrator and architect's wife all these years. They'll see her with new eyes.

Roused by these thoughts, Louisa plays a better game. She returns Kelly's savage backhand and delivers an impossible drop shot. This must be flow or whatever they call it. She's a bundle of neurons and muscle, acting and reacting. She wins the set, 6–3. Shaking Kelly's hand, she sees the sweat beads on her opponent's forehead.

"Want to go again?" Kelly says, smiling.

"Let's take five, and I'll think about it."

Earlier, she left Sylvie at the barn to be driven home by Hannah Warren's mother. Richard will be at a site visit all afternoon. Louisa had finally convinced herself that Sylvie would be all right alone for just a few hours, and Richard had reluctantly agreed. Sylvie knows the code to let herself into the house. Hannah's mother will wait in the driveway while she enters and leave only after she's safely inside. Sylvie assured them that she'd be fine. She was thrilled with the arrangement, Richard predictably less so. What if someone saw Sylvie enter the code and followed her in? What if she fell down the stairs and hit her head? What if, unsupervised, she tumbled into some internet snake pit? He told Louisa that he couldn't stop thinking of his client's daughter, showing herself to men, cushioned in her multimillion-dollar home.

Sylvie will probably be back by now. Louisa feels disquieted, thinking of it. Now that the plan is in progress, it strikes her as a bad idea. On a primal level, she wants to run home, but on a rational one, she resists. If Louisa agrees to another game with Kelly, it will allow Sylvie to be alone for at least a little while. It will give her a chance to feel the first pricks of independence and to know that Louisa trusts her.

"All right. Let's go," she says to Kelly.

The next set goes to a tiebreak, but Louisa edges out another victory. Both women are soaked by the end of it, panting and laughing as they approach the net.

"Another?" asks Louisa.

"No way, I'm done," Kelly says. "And maybe let's make it doubles next time. I'm getting too old for this."

It's only just past two when Louisa puts the tennis balls back in their tube and drives home. Sylvie will be sorry her mother is back so soon. The house is quiet as Louisa mounts the stairs, feeling the strain in her thighs. She calls Sylvie's name but hears no reply. She stands outside her daughter's bedroom door for a moment before knocking quietly. A bolt of fear shoots through her body as she knocks again and opens the door. The room is empty. Louisa walks in and stands on the braided rug.

"Sylvie?" she says quietly, as if her daughter could be under the bed.

After that, Louisa goes from room to room, calling. Clearly, unbelievably, Sylvie is not in the house. Back outside, Louisa circles the lawn. The air rattles with insects. She feels something like a goldfish flipping in her chest.

She sends a text. Her fingers tremble as she pecks out the note: *Where are you? I'm home.* She stares at the screen, waiting for the typing dots to appear. Panic is already invading her body. It's a feeling of falling, of being in an elevator whose cables are unspooling. There's no reply to her message. She calls Sylvie's phone and is sent right to voicemail. Her daughter's recorded voice in her ear sounds incredibly young, the voice of a small child.

Rosalie Warren's phone kicks her to voicemail, too, and her texts go unanswered. Louisa closes her eyes for a moment, takes a long breath, and holds it. It's possible the riding lesson has gone late, or there are barn chores to be done. Cell service at the hunt club is spotty. Calmly, she goes back out to the car and drives to the barn. Once there, she walks through the aisles, her steps echoing in the rafters. Outside, she finds girls in the lesson ring, laughing as they ride. None of the riders are Sylvie.

"I dropped her at home around noon," Rosalie says when she finally returns Louisa's call, her voice rising in alarm. "I saw her walk in the door."

"I don't understand. Where could she have gone?" Louisa says, as if to herself. "I'll try calling again."

"Please let me know when you reach her."

Back at home, Louisa makes another futile circuit through the house, as if her daughter might have been hiding all along, playing a joke. She calls again, sends another text, and goes outside. Their grass is still lush despite the prolonged drought, damp from continual sprinkling. The beach roses hold their stealth fragrance. The thought of calling the police crosses her mind, but she dismisses it. They'd treat her like a hysteric and rightfully so. These are the kinds of overwrought worries endemic to a town like this: suspicious joggers, daytime raccoons, twelve-year-olds missing for an hour.

She thinks of the woods. She looks at the trees and feels their primordial pull, the power that entraps wandering children. Sylvie's favorite spot as a little girl was a bed of ferns just beyond the tree line. That was where she'd brought the ants she rescued. Louisa steps into the trees and listens. There are no sounds, no birdcalls in the heat of the day. She shouts Sylvie's name, and before she knows what she's doing, she runs. Her lungs are already aching before she's even out of sight of the house. She trips, falls, and picks herself up with a flower of pain at the knee. Her phone has flown from her hand. As she searches for it on the ground, she hears the chirp of a text message. The sound draws her to the place where the phone lies against a tree trunk.

On my way.

Louisa's lungs still burn. Back inside the house, she collapses into a chair. The sweat has dried on her tennis clothes, and she shudders in the air-conditioning. She closes her eyes, and when she opens them several minutes later, she sees Sylvie standing outside the glass door. Her daughter silently meets her gaze before opening the door and stepping inside. She holds her head in an exaggerated attitude, chin up, as she walks past her mother without a word.

"What do you think you're doing?" Louisa says, her voice resounding in the room.

Sylvie stops.

"Where the hell were you?"

Sylvie turns, startled at this language. "I went for a walk."

"A walk? Where? I was looking for you."

Sylvie turns and moves toward the stairs, but Louisa gets up and catches her there. Up close, she notices a dirty smear on her daughter's neck and another on her forehead.

"Where did you go on this walk? What's that on your face?"

"I don't know," Sylvie murmurs.

"Where did you go?"

There's a hard backing of defiance in Sylvie's eyes. "Just the woods," she says, with a slight lilt. "Is that okay?"

Louisa examines her daughter. There's dirt caked beneath her fingernails, as if she's been digging. There's a flush in her cheeks and lips.

"That wasn't part of the plan," Louisa says, more sharply than she intends. "If you want the freedom to be left alone, you can't just leave the house and do what you want. You scared the crap out of me."

"Because I went for a walk?"

Acid rises into Louisa's throat as she digs for a retort. "That's it. You've just forfeited any chance of staying alone again."

Sylvie's mouth twitches, but she shrugs. She sidles past Louisa and goes into her bedroom, closing the door behind her.

A tide of anger rises in Louisa. She throws the door open. "Show me your phone."

Sylvie is on her bed looking up at Louisa with alarm. "Why?"

"Why? Because I'm your mother and I want to see it."

Sylvie's mouth hardens. "Fine."

Louisa takes the phone and goes out of the room. She doesn't know what she's looking for. The home screen appears, a picture of a younger Sylvie smiling beside Cracker, a red second-place ribbon hooked to his halter. Louisa jabs at the bright icons on the screen, brings up the flashing interfaces. None of the elements cohere in any recognizable way. She abandons these and punches the vibrant pink icon that looks like a camera. Here, she finds the familiar scrolling images like those she manages for the center. The pictures on Sylvie's feed are innocuous: mostly horses, some cupcakes, a few landscapes from nature nonprofits. What did she think she'd find? Did she think Sylvie would have posted swimsuit pictures of herself, like the older girls do? Did she think Sylvie spent her time secretly tallying how many people liked her pubescent body, conversing with strangers about it? Louisa knows there's another application that dissolves messages and photos within seconds, but she doesn't know what its mystical icon might look like.

She returns to Sylvie's room, where her daughter sits on the bed glaring.

"Your accounts are still set to private, right?"

"*Yes.*"

Louisa looks searchingly at her. "If I find out they're not, your phone privileges will vanish. Remember that I have a phone, too, and I can check."

"Why don't you trust me?" Sylvie's face changes as she says this. The corners of her mouth quiver as she sits on the bed, in the same spot she'd always sat for bedtime stories.

"I do," Louisa says. "It's just that my job as a parent—"

"Can I just be alone please?" Sylvie cuts her off. She curls onto the bed, facing the wall.

The three of them sit quietly for dinner. Louisa sees that there's still dirt under her daughter's nails. Sylvie appears untroubled but makes no eye contact with her mother. The flipping goldfish returns to Louisa's chest. She searches

Sylvie's face for any indication of disturbance, but again it's a mask of cool impudence.

As they eat, the green universe outside the window turns gradually bluer. Each evening comes a moment earlier now than the evening before. In a few days, Sylvie will start seventh grade. She hasn't wanted to shop for back-to-school clothing or get a new haircut. She's fine, she says, as she is.

"Sylvie, would you like to have Rachel come stay with you when we go to the gala?" Louisa asks with false brightness.

"I thought I didn't need a babysitter anymore."

"We're going to be out late, and someone needs to be here."

"I'll be fine alone."

Richard looks at Louisa.

"I'll see if Rachel's free," she says with finality.

"Everybody else gets to stay alone."

"We're not discussing it anymore."

Richard clears his throat. "So, honey, are you excited to see your friends at school?"

Sylvie shrugs.

"Well, I'm excited for you," he says, putting too much emphasis into the words. "It'll be great to be back in class, learning new things."

Louisa doesn't join this line of conversation. The flipping feeling has subsided now, replaced by a cold mass. This is how it starts, she thinks, the inevitable descent.

There's so much she's meant to discuss with Sylvie this summer before school starts again. They've gone over the basics of development and sex but not the choices and behaviors that accompany them. She hasn't yet had the chance to instill values that might counteract the corrupting undertow of peer influence. When it comes to these values, however, Louisa draws a blank. There's never a moment when Sylvie's receptive, anyway. She's become more dour, moodier than ever. It's the maelstrom of new hormones, Louisa is sure, compounded by a nature predisposed to secrecy. But maybe there's a chance it's something graver. Maybe Richard is right that Sylvie has been deeply, privately affected by Katherine's death. There are events that, if they occur at a precise moment of vulnerability in childhood, can change the design of a mind. Perhaps the shock of her friend's death has rewired hers in a way that's opened it to darker currents.

Sylvie rises from her chair, takes her dish to the kitchen, and goes upstairs to her room. Louisa knows better than to follow.

That night, Louisa and Richard talk in bed. The words he says to her and that she says to him in response, seem to roll before her like a script. Yes, they'll go away for the long weekend after the gala, as they've been vaguely planning to do. It will be good to have time together as a family, away from their routines. The summer has flown past too quickly.

They'll go to Paris. Richard will meet with his clients, and Louisa and Sylvie will sightsee. They'll find last-minute tickets someplace. It will be good for Sylvie to experience a new country, to hear a new language, to see how far the world spans beyond Nearwater. Yes, Louisa agrees, it will be good for them all.

20.

THE BOY AND girl meet each night and work by flashlight in the black velvet house. They find a switch that makes the ceiling slide open to the sky and agree that they're like the last ones on Earth, the only living pair beneath the stars. The hours pass, easy and fluid. The girl tells the boy that at the end of her book the asteroid was still on its way. Or it had already come. It was confusing, she says, but it also made perfect sense. The boy tells her that scientists have a theory. They think an asteroid may have hit our planet millions of years ago and cracked through its plates, sent up plumes of water and molten rock. There were clouds of darkness, mass extinctions. Forty days of rain. That was the basis of the flood myth.

"The piece we're making now is meant to be hopeful," the boy says. "It's going to show how the Earth will regenerate after we're gone. The planet's been around for millions of years, and in the scheme of things, humans have only been here for like five minutes. Our time's almost done. Once we've sunk into the ground, the Earth will grow over us and start again. It'll take a thousand years to get rid of all our shit, the asphalt and plastic, but eventually there'll be no sign we were ever here. All the forests and megafauna will come back. The animals will burst out and take over."

"So, it's saying that we should have hope even though there's no hope," the girl says.

The boy looks quizzically at her. He puts a hand to her cheek. "I meant to tell you. I finally finished the drawing you saw in the basement."

"Oh, can I see it?"

"I'll send it to you."

They work for three nights. First, they cover the building with sod. They peel flaps of moss from the ground at the edge of the woods and cut these into smaller squares, light enough to carry. That's the daytime work. Then, they take the moss squares one at a time to the site, carry them up the ladder, and tamp them onto the roof. They work their way down the walls with the moss, doubling up as they near the ground. This way, the slope is softened so that the structure resembles a mound. It's a lush, patchworked earth lodge, a cairn.

Lastly, they set up the laptop and projectors. After that, the boy tells the girl she can go home. "Tomorrow's a big night," he says. The rest, now, is for him to do.

21.

THE ART CENTER is transformed. Chinese lanterns color the patio blue, yellow, and pink. It's a warm September night, and while the lanterns give the atmosphere of a garden party, the frame of darkened trees lends dramatic weight. The collective vibration has dropped an octave. The guests, having exhausted their summer frippery, arrive in the more substantial fabrics and hues of gala season. Satins and lined laces. Real makeup on the women—and real jewels. A purpose to movements and comments. The sense of coming together again after a long sunburnt journey, refreshed and ready to build.

The corset leaves Louisa's shoulders bare, and despite the soft evening, she shivers. Richard, in his standard black suit, brings her a glass of champagne. At her suggestion, he's wearing a solid purple tie that saves the suit from stuffiness. Their eyes meet for a moment as she takes the glass, and she feels the catch of their first days together. How lucky she is. It's a stroke of grace that he's still here, that he still looks at her this way, that she's managed to keep it all intact. Louisa braces against the riptide of shame inside her. She smiles at her husband with true gratitude, takes a deep breath, and holds it for a moment.

Her mind keeps returning to the note she'd found on her desk that morning. Just a sentence written in black ink, a familiar scrawl: *I hope you like my gift.* She'd felt a dead bolt drop open in her, a frigid wind rush in. Ever since, she's been on edge. But now her job is to socialize. Her demeanor has to be spontaneous, sparkling. Tonight she isn't a curator but a fundraiser, a relationship builder. She buries the note away in her mind and focuses on the scene in front of her.

Among the first several couples to arrive are the Steigers, handsomely attired. Louisa's skin prickles at the sight of them. Heinrich looks particularly European—every inch the count or baron—in a bespoke suit, the jacket perfectly tapered. His wine-colored tie complements the deep blue dress on Agatha, who's more striking than ever with her hair pinned to reveal emerald earrings. In a protective instinct, Louisa turns her body a few degrees away. To her relief, two men—a couple—approach her with smiles, and Richard, bless him, leaves her side to greet the Steigers himself.

Louisa only vaguely recognizes the men, but she returns the kisses they offer her cheek. She's met so many contributors to the art center that she's given up remembering all the names. She's grateful for her years of blurry parties in

New York, which gave her practice in concealing memory blanks, made her an expert at keeping conversations both inexplicit and intent enough to pass scrutiny. "Have you seen the auction lots yet?" she asks the men brightly.

"No," the elder one says. "But we're going in to look right away."

Gretchen Von Mauren slides up to Louisa in a burnt-orange cocktail dress with the universal collar ruffle, her bespectacled husband beside her. "Oh, you've met Mark and Harris," she chirps. "Did you know that Mark helped design our renovation? He's a genius."

"Stop," the younger man says, kissing her cheek.

"Come, we have to go see the art," she commands, tugging her husband's arm. "We need something to hang in the new addition."

"Not without us, you don't," the elder man says.

"Let's all go in," Louisa says.

Inside the gallery, the sound of conversation and laughter is amplified, and Louisa lights up. After all the planning, the party is happening, people are pushing to see the art. Finally, she's at the helm of something in motion. As she maneuvers through the knots of guests in front of each piece, she allows herself a flickering fantasy that the center is becoming a cutting-edge venue—and that she's made it that way. The art on the walls tonight is far better than anything that's been exhibited in its history, a whole new caliber. No one can dispute that.

Maria Moon has agreed to donate a framed still from one of her construction-site videos, murky and portentous. Louisa has persuaded Bernard to put the screws to a couple of his artists, and to her perverse delight Angelica Ulmstead has provided something: a red ball in a glass dome, a virtual wink. Louisa smiles to see an older woman leaning down to study it. It's a good thing she'd reconnected with Angelica after all, a good thing she went to Xavier's memorial. It had all been for a purpose. A few anonymous donations from collectors have also come in. A gem of a Kara Walker sketch; a small but dreamy Wolfgang Tillmans that Louisa suspects is from the Steigers. There's even an Auguste Perren photograph, an image of a woman with horn prostheses, that's already up to $14,000.

Of course there are local donations of lesser quality but nothing horrendous. At the end of the room is Louisa's own photograph. It's a picture of the woman from the grand prix tent, in extreme close-up, the diamond earring pulling the lobe. Louisa pauses long enough to see that it already has several bids but not long enough to see the numbers, not long enough that anyone might notice her special interest. She moves on quickly. Marilyn Fox asks her about the Tillmans photograph, and Louisa enthuses over the work, the wisdom of investing in it. Several other guests join to tipsily discuss the sagacity of art investment and whether real estate is better.

"Certain hedge funds do a boutique consultation in art," Caspar Von Mauren informs them. "It's one of the safest vehicles, these days. Contemporary art, anyway. The older stuff doesn't hold value anymore."

"It's all foreign to me," Roy Fox admits. He wears a bolo tie with his suit, and Louisa sees that he's swapped his signature cowboy boots for a pair of crocodile dress shoes.

"You'll have to teach us," Marilyn says, blinking her lashes.

Louisa has promised to give an optional tour of the grounds during the cocktail hour. She wasn't certain anyone would join, but to her surprise a sizable group gathers around her on the patio at the appointed time. Chattering and laughing, they follow her onto the grass, holding their cocktail glasses. The women shriek as their spiked heels sink into the soil. A full moon hangs in the purple sky, adding to the sense of adventure as they draw farther from the patio lights and onto the path that leads through the woods. Solar lanterns planted in the ground give an uneven, pagan sort of light. As they edge into the darker provinces, the voices hush. The residency cabin is visible on the path, its windows lit.

Maria Moon welcomes them at the door, looking like a character from a fairy tale with her witchy gray hair. The guests crowd in for a viewing of her new work in progress. It's a video montage of construction sites: long shots of bulldozers silhouetted against the sky, accompanied by a thrumming techno soundtrack. Maria sits back and lights a cigarette, watching her work with a look of satisfaction. Louisa is vexed. Maria should know this is a nonsmoking space—a well-heeled suburb, not a Brooklyn warehouse. It feels like a scornful action. Louisa scans the faces of the guests for disapproval, but they're cordially watching the video. No one wants to betray prudish displeasure at the vices of a real artist, at least not in the artist's presence. Heinrich and Agatha are there, wearing opaque expressions. Louisa has still barely greeted them.

When the video is mercifully over, Louisa ushers the guests back into the fresh night air. She pulls ahead of the rest, leading them farther down the path to the audio building. As she walks, she becomes aware of a weight in her bones: from worrying over details all day, from anticipation, from not having slept well the night before. She hadn't noticed how tired she is until now. It's too early to be this tired. She'll have to push through.

The audio building is tucked away at the farthest edge of the property. Louisa hasn't been there at all recently. She's only been inside the building a handful of times since its construction, since first admiring its pitch-darkness and the way it killed all senses but hearing. She remembers the first time she touched the plush new walls and watched the ceiling slide open.

Richard comes up beside her as they approach the place in the woods where the building is hidden. "We really should bring Sylvie out here with a telescope sometime," he says. "We missed the Perseid meteor shower last month."

"Oh, that's a shame."

"The Leonids are in November. Let's try to remember."

The group winds around the last few trees to where the audio building hides. For a moment, Louisa thinks they've gone the wrong way. The building isn't where it should be. There's something else in its place, a colossal mound of turf. The mound towers in front of them like a shaggy green beast. It's so unexpected, so bizarre that Louisa stops walking. There's something almost druidic about it. It's like a ceremonial space that predates them all, that somehow she'd never noticed before—or that has manifested on its own without explanation.

"So interesting," someone comments behind her.

"Wow, I love it," a woman croons.

"Louisa, whose work is this?" someone else asks.

Louisa feels a chill. She gives her most inscrutable smile and nods toward the mound as if it will answer for itself.

"Oh, look at *that*," someone remarks, pointing.

It takes a moment for Louisa to notice that just above the mound's door hangs the antlered skull of a deer. It strikes her as menacing, like a sentry above the mouth of a tomb. No one else seems thrown. They all assume it's a new site-specific installation that's been prepared for them, an unexpected delight. A man approaches the door, opens it, and lets the woman behind him go in first. Louisa stands back. She doesn't want to go near it.

Several minutes later, the first woman reemerges with an agitated look on her face, which she replaces with an affected expression of wonderment. As the next guests pass her to enter, she glances at Louisa and then away. People enter and exit. Clusters form, and low voices create a sizzling static. No one approaches Louisa.

"What's in there?" Richard asks her.

All her nerves fire at once in animal alarm. She flashes a small smile at her husband and moves toward the building. The guests seemed to have settled on entering singly or in pairs. As Louisa waits her turn, her mind plays a dripping, gruesome horror show of Bosch, Bacon. She goes in alone.

She sees that the round room is illuminated by video projections that cover the entirety of the curving black wall. They create a moving image of a dim forest: trees reaching to the ceiling, leaves animated by breeze. It's a disconcerting feeling at first, coming indoors from the woods to an identical setting. But there's also a peaceful sublimity, as if entering a church. Beneath this, a sinister thread weaves, a sense of being entrapped, observed. A gust goes through Louisa—the same mix of pleasure, confusion, and dread delivered by any new and unusual work of art.

Slowly, she realizes that there's sound too. At first, it's a quiet shifting of branches, then a cracking of twigs, as if someone or something is moving past. Then, human sounds.

There's a rustling of fabric, ragged breaths, followed by a louder, sharp gasp. Louisa, standing in the room, feels herself losing air. The audio loop continues around her, the gasps escalating to moans. The volume rises. She clearly hears her own voice, saying his name, and his voice murmuring hers. At the last moment, at the highest octave of fever, the trees explode into flames. For several seconds, Louisa is surrounded by fire. Then the audio cuts out and the room goes black.

She stands in darkness. It's as if she's floating in some astral anteroom, untethered to Earth. Her head feels enormous and light, wanting to rise away from her body. Time seems to fold inward, and she suddenly suspects that she's dreaming, that no one is gathered outside the building, that the gala has yet to occur. She'll wake any minute and start the morning anew. For a suspended moment, she almost believes this to be true. Then the projectors, which she now understands to be rigged to the ceiling, click back on. The trees reappear. The sounds begin again, low at first. She rushes to where she remembers the door to be.

She bursts back out into the night, into the congregation of trees and gala guests. Through her spinning vision, she sees Richard. Their eyes meet. Her face must betray something because his look changes, goes from questioning concern to rigidity, as if armoring itself. In a corner of her mind, she considers grabbing his arm, pulling him away from the building. She thinks of announcing to the crowd that the piece has been damaged and can't be viewed. An idea flashes in her, to go back and ruin the piece herself, but how can she slash through light and sound? The projectors are inaccessible. She wouldn't even be able to find the electrical outlet in the dark.

Richard turns away and enters the audio room.

She stands and waits. The guests murmur around her. While her husband is out of sight, she's overtaken by a peculiar sense of calm. She looks at the people talking together in their small groups. As time passes, the muted timbre of their conversations begins to lift. Their voices return to normal volume, and there are a few volleys of laughter. After several minutes, the line to enter the audio room has grown. Richard must have stayed for two or three video loops already.

Finally, a woman pulls away from a cluster and comes up to Louisa. Gretchen Von Mauren, wearing a crooked smile. "That was unexpected," she says coyly.

At this moment, Richard exits the building and comes directly toward Louisa, where she stands with Gretchen. As he approaches, Louisa looks at the woman. She sees the earrings and the lipsticked mouth, the colored hair and the costume of raw silk. She sees the made-up eyelids and lashes. Of every part of this woman, only the irises are bare. They wait nakedly for Louisa's response, her breakdown or denial. Louisa can't read the woman's eyes in the dark, but she's sure that if she could, she'd glimpse mildewed chambers in them, buried cavities of need that she herself doesn't know are there.

As Richard approaches, some wire inside Louisa touches another. All at once, they ignite and throw light. She sees clearly.

"Did you like it?" she asks Gretchen. "I call it *Burn Risk*."

A mystified look passes over the woman's face. The next instant, it's replaced with something else. Fear. Respect. She glances at Richard, who stands between them.

"Yes, I did like it," she says. "At first, I was confused, a little unsettled, to be honest. It's quite startling. Powerful."

"Thank you," Louisa replies.

Richard stands silently. Gretchen Von Mauren glances at him again, then retreats to her cluster.

After she's gone, Richard says, "I'm going home."

"Richard."

He looks at Louisa in a way she's never seen. The natural warmth has left his face. Other guests continue taking turns in the audio room. Out of the corner of her eye, she sees the Steigers go in.

"Richard, please, don't overreact."

"How can you say that?"

"It's an art piece. It's art."

He studies her face, then turns and walks away.

She follows, extending her stride to avoid having to run. The others are watching. He doesn't acknowledge her, and she doesn't speak, but she walks alongside him, keeping pace. Like this, they return over the wooded paths to the main building. Richard doesn't enter the building but instead circles around to the parking lot. Louisa lets him go. From her place on the grass, she sees the headlights sweep past.

At dinner, everyone talks about the audio room. Only the Steigers are conspicuously reserved. Agatha is grim at the table next to Louisa's, ignoring Harold Christensen seated beside her. Louisa avoids looking at either her or Heinrich. She herself is wedged between two guests who hadn't been on the tour: Carol Christensen and an elderly gentleman whose family has been in Nearwater since the nineteenth century. She remains stubbornly attentive to these companions. As Carol talks, Louisa studies the granules of her mulberry lipstick, the face powder like pollen. To look away from Carol's face, to look toward the Steigers even once, would be fatal. It's a blessing that the old Nearwater man carries on a slow monologue about his family history and that the conversation with Carol is impenetrably bland, about her surgeries and vacation houses. Louisa wouldn't be able to survive anything deeper than the appeals of the North Fork versus the Hamptons and whether Shelter Island is worth the ferry ride. The installation already seems like a hallucination. If others hadn't been there, Louisa might have thought it had sprung from her own imagination, from her own cache of shame.

At last, Deirdre comes through the room, slick as a seal in her black vinyl dress, with the results of the art auction in hand. Louisa glances through the lot numbers and sees that her own photograph has been purchased for $1,200 by Mark Tilley and Harris Garrett. She should be pleased. They're influencers, the kind of people who could swing her name into play. She should go to their table and talk to them. To rise in the art world, half the battle is nurturing relationships with collectors, remaining in view. But she can't leave her seat. Marilyn Fox approaches her table, saying how dismayed she is that she and Roy missed the tour.

"I hear it was tremendous," she says.

Louisa smiles tightly, tells her that she's welcome to come back for a private tour sometime. Harold Christensen, to her relief, hasn't interrogated her about the surprise in the woods but seems gratified by what he's heard of its furtive subversion, which has gotten the guests talking. That, after all, is why they hired her.

Louisa checks her phone surreptitiously whenever there's a break in conversation, hoping for a message from Richard. It takes every atom of control to stay seated and ask insipid questions of Carol Christensen, to keep her talking until, at last, the dinner plates are cleared. The end of the evening is almost in sight. She stands to take the list of auction results to the microphone for her speech of gratitude. As she rises to her feet, she feels the concentrated focus of the guests, the hundreds of appraising eyes. The floor dips beneath her. Video projectors switch on, splashing the art center logo over the walls to accompany the finale—and the logo spirals and throbs strobe-like around her. She fights her way toward the microphone, as if walking over the deck of a moving sailboat. When she finally steps onto the platform, she hears the crack of applause.

22.

"**S**HE WAS IN bed," the babysitter keens when Richard
arrives home. "I said good night to her and came
back downstairs. I was sitting right here on the couch,
and I didn't hear anything the whole time. I just went up a
minute ago to check on her, and she was gone. I don't know
how she got out without me noticing."

"Why didn't you call?"

"I was going to, but I thought she must be in the house,
and I didn't want to worry you for no reason."

Richard battles the urge to shake the girl. He looks at her
and sees stupidity in her face—the low forehead and round,
frightened eyes, the pimples covered with makeup, the lip
gloss and overbrushed hair. Who is she primping for on a
babysitting job? Her hands flutter uselessly as she talks. She
keeps saying, "I'm so sorry, it's all my fault." He tells her in
a controlled voice: "It's not your fault." But it is. What she
hasn't mentioned, which he knows to be true, is that she may
have been physically on the couch, but she hadn't been in

the house. She'd been absent, deep in the playroom of her phone. Watching videos with those white buds stuck in her ears. Or taking pictures of herself pouting with her glossed mouth. Sylvie could easily have come down the stairs and gone out the front door without arousing her notice. They'd have been better off hiring a border collie.

His calls and texts to Sylvie's phone go unanswered, so he sets off in the Jaguar to look for her. The search is futile, driving in circles, scanning the side of the road. All the while, the trees mock him. It's as if he's still in the audio room, unable to leave. Each conscious moment is encased in a scrim of panic about his daughter, but a trench is also opening beneath the surface, a deep, cold place where his wife has fallen.

He returns to the house to wait. The babysitter breaks into tears, gasping for breath, and Richard wants to scream. Finally, he tells her to go home. He tries to put kindness in his voice as he tells her there's no need for her to stay. He doesn't pay her.

When the knock comes, Richard's blood stops. He opens the door to two firefighters. They aren't here about Sylvie, thank the Lord. A wildfire has begun spreading in the woods they say, not far from this area. Even if evacuation isn't necessary, it's better to be safe. Their message doesn't penetrate at first. It seems immaterial, an improbable story. Yet Richard is shaken in the presence of these men. They're snap decision makers, reactors, trained on instinct. He, in contrast, lives in the land of the long term, a land of designing and drafting. He works slowly, with pencil and paper. His projects take years to plan and execute, each a new pinnacle born of education and experience. But looking into the ruddy faces of the firefighters, he realizes the utter vanity of it all. He understands that every one of his tools, all his care and delicacy, are impotent in the face of fire. These gruff men, with their rubber suits and unwieldy hoses, are—have always been—the only bulwark against calamity. They inform him that he needs to take his tools, his flimsy plans, and move aside.

As they turn to leave, Richard hurriedly tells them that his daughter is at large, and they give him a long look, something between indifference and pity. They'll keep an eye out, they say. Alone again, he feels a cramp in his stomach. It's a sharp pain just beneath the ribs at the diaphragm, and it occurs to him that it might be angina. People have heart attacks without realizing it, thinking it's indigestion. In the bathroom, he feels his face turn cold and clammy. His phone trills. Sylvie.

All good, coming home.

When the event is over, Louisa leaves Deirdre and the others to wrap up the auction, pairing the artworks with their winners. It's midnight by the time she drives home. Her body feels hollow, hardened with fatigue, and she finds herself jerking the wheel to avoid dark baubles that loop in front of her eyes. Around a bend, a solid shape darts low across the road—something real emerging from the woods—and she thinks she glimpses the white-tipped tail of a fox.

She comes into the house to find Richard in his office stuffing papers in a suitcase. Blueprints, tax returns, passports. He doesn't look up when she enters.

"We're under evacuation orders," he tells her without inflection. "Go grab whatever you want to take with you. I don't know how long we have."

"What?"

"There's a wildfire in the woods. The fire department was here."

Louisa stares at him. "A wildfire? Where?"

"I don't know, Louisa. Just go pack your things."

Louisa feels an icy rod form in her chest as she hurries up the stairs. She doesn't stop to consider the ramifications of what Richard has said or to question him further. Sylvie is awake in her bedroom, she sees, gathering whatever minutiae she values most. Louisa goes to her own closet. She pulls out a jacket and tennis sneakers and puts them in a big tote. She adds pajamas and a few of her best dresses. As she moves, she finds herself thinking of the other gala guests, who will have been home for a while now. They will have taken off their formal wear and gotten into bed already. Only the Raders are being prevented from resting. This feels true, even as she knows that it isn't. She knows

that at this same moment their neighbors must be collecting their valuables as well. Yet, it feels as if this evacuation
order, this fire, is aimed at them specifically. Some power
has chosen them—or her—for punishment. She drops
her whole jewelry chest into the tote. Last, she pulls the
portfolios from their burrow and carries them in her arms.
The ice in her chest radiates outward, numbing her skin.
She breathes deeply against the fear that these may be the
last moments in her home.

Back downstairs, she reports to Richard's office like an
obedient child.

"Sylvie wasn't here when I got back," he tells her, facing
away. "The babysitter was hysterical."

"What do you mean she wasn't here? Where was she?"

"She said she was at the barn. She said she'd forgotten to
feed Cracker. It was her job to feed him today." He turns
toward Louisa for the first time but doesn't meet her eye. "I
didn't know the girls fed the horses."

Louisa stares. "I didn't think they did."

"She didn't want to tell the babysitter because she was
afraid she wouldn't be allowed to go. Apparently, she snuck
out of the house and rode her bike there."

"She rode her bike to the barn in the dark?"

"That's what she said."

"Do you believe her?"

Richard's eyes move to something over Louisa's shoulder,
and she turns to see Sylvie in the doorway. Her daughter

stands, pallid and large-eyed, in an old horse-print nightshirt that barely covers her. Faintly, Louisa hears the sound of distant sirens.

"It must be a big fire," Sylvie says in a strange, choked voice.

The sound of sirens comes nearer, and a physical surge passes through Louisa, fight or flight. She looks at Richard.

"I think we should go now," he states.

There's only one hotel in town. Richard takes the driver's seat and together they go toward it. He jams the brakes to avoid a pair of deer vaulting in front of the car. The sirens grow increasingly louder, and as they turn onto the next street, they finally see the trucks, emergency lights wheeling. A row of orange cones blocks the road. It's shocking to see this scene so near, on the same road Louisa has just driven from the art center. At least if the fire is near the big estates they'll move heaven and earth to stop it.

A firefighter stands among the cones, waving his arms. The smell of smoke has intensified, the haze moving visibly in the air. The young man comes to Richard's window.

"We've got a wildfire this way. You're gonna have to leave the area." There's controlled excitement and fear in his voice, and Louisa has the sense this is his first big event.

"We know. We're on our way out."

"Which way is it going?" Louisa asks from the passenger seat.

"Appears to be heading due south toward Edgewood, but the wind could change."

"The art center's on Edgewood. Have you evacuated there?"

The young firefighter stares for a moment.

"There's a resident on the property," Louisa hears her voice rise in pitch. She's thinking about Maria but also Gabriel. She knows it's impossible that he'd be in the cabin, but she feels suddenly certain of it, and a shrill ringing comes into her ears. "I don't know if the resident stayed overnight or not, but she could be there. Has anyone looked for occupants on the property? There are several outbuildings."

The firefighter turns and yells to the men near the trucks. The men turn, and he goes toward them, shouting.

"Oh my God," Louisa whispers.

There's more shouting among the men, and three of them set off at a military run into the woods. Louisa turns and sees Sylvie in the back seat with wet eyes. All at once, she feels the delayed relief of having her daughter here, safe. "Are you all right, honey?" she asks.

"I'm not crying. It's the smoke," Sylvie says.

The young firefighter returns, shaking his head. "I'm sorry, but you can't stay here. You're going to have to leave the area."

"I need to know about the resident," Louisa says. "I'm the director of the art center. Her safety is my responsibility."

"It's our responsibility now. Thank you for alerting us, and we'll make sure everyone's safe," the firefighter says in a firm, unconvincing tone.

Louisa's throat is almost fully closed. Her ears still ring so that the sounds of approaching fire engines come to her through gauze. Their lights spin in the dark. She hears Richard's voice faintly, as if from a distance. He's asking the firefighter: "Do you think the whole area's really in danger?"

No, it's impossible, she wants to answer. These houses are too solid, too shielded to burn. There are rock walls, watered lawns, swimming pools. They're made of stone, brick, glass. Their own house is untouchable, built for the ages.

"We're doing our best to control it," the young man answers.

"Let's go," Louisa whispers.

They take a detour into town, away from the commotion. Their headlights carve a limited path in front of them, illuminating the smoke in the air. The full moon has, at some point in the night, slipped behind cloud cover and the world is black all around, the blackest night Louisa can remember. It's like driving through a tunnel. She thinks of officers knocking on the doors of the darkened homes, ringing doorbells that peal through the rooms of palaces. These people aren't used to being disturbed from their sleep. Theirs is the sleep of the sated, the sovereign. Or maybe she's wrong—maybe they sleep lightly, like she does, primed to wake at the first sound of an intruder. Maybe they've been anticipating this moment.

Richard swerves. "Raccoon, I think. They're coming out of the woods."

He slows the car and puts the high beams on. His face is set, jaw set. He still hasn't looked at Louisa.

"Jesus," he says, swerving again.

Again, an animal darts in front of them. It isn't a raccoon or opossum but rather a primate-like thing with reddish fur. It turns its face toward them as it leapfrogs over the road, a black mask with flashing eyes. Richard is driving too slowly now. She wants to ask him to hurry, to take them out of this haunted tunnel. Another animal comes out that none of them recognize, a large, furred rodent that shuffles on the side of the road. Louisa feels suffocated, trapped in an airless grotto. She leans back against the leather headrest and closes her eyes.

Finally, they reach the center of town, the deserted strip of the Post Road.

"Stoplight's out," Richard says, advancing slowly through the empty intersection.

Louisa lifts her head weakly. The traffic light hangs lifeless, three black eyes. They glide down the road, past the dormant shops. The hotel is at the end of the strip. It alone has lit windows. The roar of a generator fills the lobby as the frazzled night clerk checks them in. They pay for a deluxe room: a king bed and a sleeper sofa for Sylvie. Their window on the fifth floor gives a panoramic view of town and of the malefic orange light pulsing in the distance.

Louisa lies awake in the hotel bed for a long time. Richard faces away from her. Whether he's asleep or not she can't tell. Sylvie is silent in the foldout bed, although she keeps changing position, shifting on her pillow. Louisa's head throbs with images from the evening: the decorated guests, the artwork on the walls, the woman with prosthetic horns, the blazing trees, Richard's stony face. Although the hotel's generator isn't audible, she thinks she can feel its vibration through the wall. She thinks she can still hear the screaming sirens outside, like banshees portending doom. Her pillow is too firm, overstuffed. An ache begins in her neck and tension invades her jaw. She finds a nighttime pain reliever and waits for it to kick in, but her muscles won't loosen. Her mind won't slow.

At some point in the night, thunder rolls. Gradually, it strides closer, an invisible giant. Finally, it stamps and crashes overhead, and a flash of lightning illuminates Sylvie as she bolts upright in bed. Louisa waits for her to call out, to climb up and nestle between her parents, as she so often did as a small child. Instead, she stays in place and waits through the next thundercrack, then settles back under the sheets. The grumbling thunder withdraws, and Louisa hears the rainstorm that follows. It comes down hard, like a bombardment of stones. She hears it pummel the roof of the hotel and the cars in the parking lot below. She lies awake and listens, imagining the downpour battering the town, hammering their house, the Steigers' house, the earthen audio building. She imagines the fire receding in the woods, shrinking under the punishment of water.

23.

THE NEARWATER TRAIN station is on the New Haven line, an hour's commute to Grand Central. The station itself is the quaint original, periodically refinished, although its service window has permanently closed in favor of ticket machines. The boy stands alone on the platform, waiting for the midnight train. The houses near the tracks are dark. There's only a faint smell of smoke, a complaint of distant sirens. At last, the train shows its head around the bend and slides its body into view. It screeches to a stop and the doors open. The boy steps inside.

He sits alone under the stark fluorescent lights. In the window, his reflection looks back at him. As the train begins moving, he aims his phone at the window, where his shadowed face flickers. He tries a few times until he captures an image of himself imposed on the blurred platform lights, just as the train passes the Nearwater sign. He sends it to the girl. Then he finds a photograph in his camera roll, a pencil portrait of her on horseback in medieval armor, gaze cast up to the sky. *Thank you, my Joan of Arc. Here's the drawing I promised.*

He leans back in his seat and watches Nearwater slide past the train window. The streetlights pick up speed and then, all at once, they blink out. The world outside the window turns black. He sees only his own face, his own eyes in the glass.

24.

LTHOUGH THE DOWNPOUR has finally quenched the wildfire, electricity doesn't return to Nearwater until the next afternoon. When the Raders leave their hotel in the morning, there's chaos on the Post Road, the stoplights crippled. Cars honk and swerve. Police are everywhere, but their numbers are inadequate to quell the confusion. The Raders return to find their own house mercifully untouched. The trees at the property's edge appear sound.

According to the local news, the fire had originated at the Fox estate. The bulk of damage has been on the north side of town. They learn that the Fox mansion has been all but destroyed; only the stone exterior remains. No one, thankfully, had been on the premises at the time. The main gate had been opened, and the animals had somehow gotten free. The grounds are charred, the gardens ravaged. The fire progressed so quickly that it had overwhelmed the fire department's capabilities. Several neighboring houses had been badly damaged, and over three hundred acres had burned before the rainstorm came to the rescue. Most of the animals had been captured and brought to zoos for temporary care. The Bengal tiger was found on the grounds of the high school and safely sedated. But there have been sightings of strange marsupials in gardens. Several golden lion tamarins remain missing, and the anteater is unaccounted for.

There's no clear explanation for how the fire might have started. Arson is being investigated, and members of the Foxes' staff are being questioned. The owners tell reporters that they will rebuild their sanctuary.

Louisa realizes how lucky they are. The fire had come close. It could easily have gone a different way. On their return, the house feels changed, disrobed somehow. They can smell burnt wood, even from indoors. Both Richard and Sylvie have gone upstairs for naps. Louisa is also exhausted but can't think of lying down yet. She busies herself in the kitchen to tame her overcharged nerves, washing and drying the dishes and glasses that were left out before the gala, a hundred years ago. She'd had a glass of her favorite California chardonnay before leaving. There'd been about a quarter of a bottle remaining. It's only just past noon, but Louisa thinks she might finish it now. Strangely, the bottle isn't where she'd left it on the counter or in the recycling bin. It's possible the babysitter might have helped herself to a sip or two, but she'd have known better than to take the whole thing. Louisa checks the cabinets and refrigerator in vain.

When she finally goes upstairs, she finds Richard with his business suitcase on the bed. He's already filled it with shirts and trousers.

"I've decided to go to Paris early," he tells her before she can ask. "I'm going to meet with the Lenoirs and stay to supervise the project. I'll be gone for a few weeks."

"A few weeks?"

He looks up at her. "I need some time, Louisa."

She doesn't speak.

"Obviously you understand that."

"No," she says.

He looks at her dispassionately. "Maybe it's my fault. I should have known this would happen someday. You're a child."

She takes a step toward him and breathes deeply. "But I told you. It's art."

He slaps the suitcase closed. "What does that even mean?"

She doesn't answer. Richard leaves the bedroom and knocks on Sylvie's door. Louisa doesn't follow, doesn't know what Richard says to their daughter. He comes back out a few minutes later and goes down the stairs with the suitcase. Louisa follows wordlessly. Before she can think of how to stop him, he's gone.

For a long time, Louisa sits in the living room, on the white couch. The smell of smoke is still in her clothes. The house is silent. The tall windows form a cylinder around her—the daytime contrast to the audio room's round night.

Looking through them, she views the flat grass, the indifferent trees already dropping their leaves. It's a bright September day, the sun a white star.

There's no sound from upstairs. Sylvie might be sleeping or sobbing. Louisa thinks of going to her room but can't seem to initiate the motions of standing. Richard will already be on the highway by now, on his way to the regional airport that connects with the international hub in the city. Louisa has always liked their small airport. There's never a line for security, and after passing through the metal detector, passengers are treated to a view of the runway through a vast window. Soon, Richard's plane will be speeding outside that window, lifting off the ground. Louisa imagines its wheels losing contact with pavement, the space between airplane and earth widening until the jet is aloft.

She closes her eyes. For a moment, she tries to remember the smell of old books in the stalls near the Seine. It's been twenty years since she last saw Paris, since she went with regularity for fashion shoots. She remembers walking at dusk past mysterious women on benches, exhaling smoke like river mist from their mouths. The city will be changed now, of course. She thinks of Notre-Dame in ruins under scaffolding and remembers her first visit, marveling at its famous rose window, naturally imbuing the lacework with her own boundless promise of youth.

Louisa's reverie is broken by a clatter overhead and the sound of Sylvie rushing downstairs. She says something that sounds like: "Look at all the rabbits," as she blurs past her mother in the living room and goes out the front door.

A moment later, Sylvie is outside. From where she sits, Louisa sees her daughter through the window, creeping on the lawn in her nightshirt. Louisa remains in position on the couch, unmoving. The smell from her own clothing has become increasingly repellent: smoke mixed with sweat and something else, something acrid. Maybe adrenaline, some pungent off-gas of terror. As she watches Sylvie, an intuition ripples deep inside her like a dusky flag. Without thinking, she follows its directive, standing from the couch and climbing the stairs to Sylvie's bedroom.

The room looks the same. Long-neglected stuffed animals are still in their baskets, baby dolls in their bassinets. The horse show ribbons are still strung up, ordered by color, collecting dust. The only object Louisa doesn't recognize is a hand-painted clay figure of a tiger on the dresser. On the bed is the blanket Louisa had chosen for Sylvie after she graduated from a crib: dark blue with hundreds of stars in no natural order. When Sylvie was younger, she'd trace shapes among them, inventing new designs: the rabbit, the horse, the bear. Always animals. That's what people always see, Louisa supposes. Even the world is carried on the back of a turtle, according to the earliest myth.

Sylvie's clothes from the past week are in the hamper. Louisa picks up the things she'd been wearing the day before. As she examines the shirt—black cotton with the word "artist" printed in purple—a sharp odor meets her nose. It takes a moment for her brain to identify the smell of gasoline. Everything stinks of it: the shirt, the jeans, the socks. Louisa drops the clothes back into the hamper and moves to the dresser where Sylvie has left her phone. She presses the home button and is confronted with a keypad. A newly installed passcode. Heat rises to her face. Without thinking, she enters 1-2-3-4, then 4-3-2-1. She realizes she's holding her breath. She inhales deeply and enters the digits of Sylvie's birthday. The keypad disappears.

Standing in the bedroom, she goes through the apps with their maddening, mysterious graphics. Her breath comes quickly now, uneven. She hits every button and link, which lead to more buttons and links. Richard's client, desperately tracking his daughter, might have been lost in a maze like this too. Parents, even those who think they know, don't know. They don't know where to look in the maze. They don't know about the hidden folds.

Finally, she quits the apps and opens the photo roll. The most recent pictures are familiar, taken at the hotel. She recognizes the pattern of the carpet in their room. The continental breakfast in the lobby dining room, the television screen in the corner, the newscaster reporting on the fire. Artistic photos. Interesting angles, unusual compositions. As she scrolls up, the pictures change. There's a series of dark images. It's hard to make out what they are. An attempt to capture the night sky, maybe, or to photograph the moon.

Only a few appear to have any discernible form. In one of them, she makes out the dim contours of a young man. He appears to be facing away, with an object in his hand, shaped like a bottle.

She swipes to the next image and zooms in. As she studies it, the image resolves into a picture of an animal at night, its eyes like golden disks in the camera flash. It looks back at her. A hunted thing, a thing that's been waiting all along.

When Louisa comes back downstairs, she sees that Sylvie is still outside on the lawn. She stands and watches her daughter. There are at least five rabbits nearby, brown and trembling, hunched close to the ground. Sylvie hunches, too, stepping softly, a few inches at a time, trying to draw near. For a long time, Louisa stands at the window, feeling the chill of the indoor air. For a long time, she watches her daughter stalking the grass, the rabbits fretting.

Acknowledgments

Thank you to all at Grove Atlantic for bringing this book to life, especially Katie Raissian for her editorial brilliance, the excellent Elisabeth Schmitz, Kait Astrella, Deb Seager, Judy Hottensen, Natalie Church, Rachel Gilman, Andrew Unger, Ian Dreiblatt, Paula Cooper Hughes, Julia Berner-Tobin, Gretchen Mergenthaler, Morgan Entrekin, and the whole dream team, with gratitude as ever to the late Virginia Barber. Enduring thanks to everyone at the Clegg Agency, and to Bill Clegg for championing this story—and me—from the nascent beginning. I'm indebted to all who read drafts: Thomas Doyle, Melissa Hile, Emily Mitchell, Sara Shepard, and Emily Takoudes. Gratitude to the Ragdale Foundation, the Ucross Foundation, and Art Omi for time, space, and validation. Love and thanks to my mother, Mary Ann Acampora, to Tom and Linda Doyle, and to Thomas and Amity, always.